My darling Remy,

What a Twelfth Night this has turned out to be!

I should have never tempted fate by asking what else could go wrong the night of the blackout. I'm beginning to believe that trouble really does come in threes. First the power outage, then the generator failure and now a dead woman in one of our courtyard rooms.

No one seems to know who the poor woman is, and the police are investigating, but you can imagine how disturbing this has been for the guests and the staff. But as we always used to say, mon cher, we have been truly blessed with our daughters, and likewise with our staff. You would especially appreciate our new concierge, Luc. He has done so much for the hotel since his arrival, and has been so supportive through all the difficulties we have been facing recently. The guests adore him, and he's willing to help whenever—wherever—we need him.

So with a wonderful family and a loyal staff, it would be wrong of me to worry. I have to believe that things will get better for our Hotel Marchand. We built it with love—what could be stronger?

Missing you as always,

Anne

Dear Reader,

While in New Orleans for a writing conference, I researched the city during every spare minute between workshops. I loved exploring the museums, touring the famous French Quarter and—I couldn't believe my luck—meeting a retired steamboat captain. We were both having beignets and coffee near the river and I just had to ask about his uniform and the captain's bars on the shoulders. Talk about good juju! He played the calliope on one of the river queens three days a week and invited me to ride along. The captain and I stood on the roof of the steamboat while he played an electronic keyboard connected to the calliope. I felt like a homecoming queen as the big paddle wheel churned and pushed us up the river, leaving a white wake and trail of music behind us.

Cost of airline ticket to get to New Orleans? I don't remember. Food and lodging? I can't recall. Standing on the roof of the steamboat with a handsome older man and waving at the crowd? Priceless!

Laurie Paige

LAURIE PAIGE
The Unknown Woman

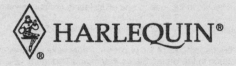

HARLEQUIN®

TORONTO • NEW YORK • LONDON
AMSTERDAM • PARIS • SYDNEY • HAMBURG
STOCKHOLM • ATHENS • TOKYO • MILAN • MADRID
PRAGUE • WARSAW • BUDAPEST • AUCKLAND

ISBN-13: 978-0-373-38940-7
ISBN-10: 0-373-38940-X

THE UNKNOWN WOMAN

Laurie Paige reports that she is working on her seventieth romance book. She is still married to her high school sweetheart. It's cold and snowy in the mountains of northern California where she lives, but when she checks the weather news on TV, she notes the temperatures in New Orleans and other cities that got hit by Hurricane Katrina. While many people have found refuge in other states, she knows that, in the landscape of the heart, there's no place like home.

CHAPTER ONE

KERRY JOHNSTON STUDIED the brochures on New Orleans that she'd picked up that morning. Here she was, having lunch in the famous French Quarter, and she was feeling down. This trip was supposed to cheer her up after the difficult year she'd just had, not leave her feeling more lonely than ever.

The restaurant she'd chosen, up the street from the Hotel Marchand where she was staying, had a charming Old World atmosphere and seemed bustling after the slump caused by the devastation of Hurricane Katrina.

Fortunately this area of the city was higher than districts west of the river and hadn't suffered as much flood damage. She surveyed the historic buildings with their lovely fretwork of iron lace. They reminded Kerry of elderly ladies dressed in their finest outfits, waiting for gentlemen callers.

She winced. Maybe that would be a description of *her* one day.

Well, she didn't feel old and she wasn't waiting for anyone, but she sure wished she didn't feel so blue.

"Here you are."

The waitress, dressed simply in black slacks and a crisp white shirt, expertly placed a huge salad, complete with crayfish and a secret house dressing, in front of Kerry.

The woman's name tag read Patti, and she was truly beautiful, with blue eyes and the blackest lashes Kerry had ever seen. Her smile was infectious, and her complexion, a blend of tan and rose, was flawless.

By contrast, Kerry felt rather plain with her short spiky light brown hair and hazel eyes, her face pale from the Midwest winter.

The waitress was at least ten years younger than Kerry, maybe twenty-five. She looked vivacious and happy with her life, and on her finger was a gold ring with an intricate rope design.

From a lover? Kerry wondered. She sighed inwardly as her gaze drifted to her bare ring finger. Last summer an engagement diamond had sparkled there.

"Are you here for Mardi Gras?" the waitress asked in a friendly manner, placing a glass of iced tea and a basket of hot rolls on the table.

"Well, not the whole season," Kerry replied, returning the smile. "I have a week. The trip was a birthday present from my friends back home."

"How nice of them. Where do these friends live? Perhaps I can meet them?"

Her soft laughter was enchanting. This woman was exotic and beautiful enough to be a movie star.

Kerry felt as stale as day-old bread. "White Bear Lake, Minnesota—a tiny place that no one's ever heard of. It's near the St. Paul–Minneapolis area."

"It sounds charming," Patti said.

"Are you a native of New Orleans?" Kerry asked, thinking her accent and manner of speaking suggested that.

"*Mais oui.*"

"Creole?" Kerry asked, smiling at the obvious pride in the lilting voice. From a TV documentary, she knew those of Creole descent often prided themselves on speaking fluent French without the patois of the Cajun population.

"Yes. My people have been here a long time. We are descended from the same line as Empress Josephine, who was born, as my own ancestors were, on Martinique. My family moved to Louisiana. She married Vicomte Alexandre de Beauharnais, son of the French governor of the island, and lived in Paris."

"Where she met and later wed Napoleon Bonaparte after her estranged husband was executed," Kerry concluded, recalling her history lessons.

Patti's eyes sparked with delight. "It's a romantic story, is it not?"

"Except possibly from the *Vicomte's* view," Kerry said drolly, causing Patti to laugh.

A couple came and sat down at the next table.

"Enjoy your lunch," Patti said, then turned to attend the new guests.

Kerry wasn't sure whether the waitress's story about her ancestors was true or a put-on for the tourists, but she found it interesting. Just as she had been cast aside for another woman, Josephine Bonaparte had been replaced by a younger woman who could give the emperor an heir.

At least Ben had married someone her own age, Kerry thought, a divorced classmate who'd returned to town for their high school reunion. Kerry's fiancé of four years had fallen for Marla like a "ton of bricks," as he'd so eloquently—and rather shamefacedly—explained.

It turned out he'd had a crush on her their entire senior year and the flame had rekindled the minute he'd seen her again. Kerry had said she understood and returned his ring, freeing him to find happiness with his new love.

Since then, she'd often wondered if a four-year engagement should have told her something. Neither of them had been in a hurry to make that final commitment.

With a philosophical shrug, she determinedly put the past behind her. That had been in July. This was January.

In fact, it was Twelfth Night, the very beginning of the Mardi Gras celebration. Actually, her friends had wanted to get her a reservation on her birthday, Valentine's Day, but the hotels were booked solid then.

She glanced heavenward, thankful for small favors. Being alone in New Orleans—the most haunted city in the U.S., according to the brochures, and certainly one of the most romantic—on Valentine's Day, her birthday, would have been too much.

Blinking away sudden tears, she sipped the iced tea until she was over the attack of self-pity. When she finished the meal, which was delicious, she reviewed the brochures once more, annoyed by her inability to make a decision about what to do.

"Have you been to the voodoo museum?" Patti asked, pausing at Kerry's table after serving salads and drinks to the couple. "Most visitors seem to enjoy it." She glanced at her watch. "You should go there this afternoon if you're free. From two until three is usually a good time. The museum is quieter then."

"Thanks. That sounds like the perfect place to begin sightseeing on my first day in New Orleans."

"Have fun," the waitress said brightly before sailing off once more to attend to her customers.

After leaving a generous tip, Kerry left the restaurant and wandered around Jackson Square and the streets of the French Quarter. Going into a tourist shop, she checked out various voodoo-related souvenirs with her nephew and two nieces in mind.

Poor kids. They all had chicken pox. Her sister Sharon was supposed to be on this trip with her, but when the kids got sick, she'd had to stay at home. Shane, Kerry's eleven-year-old nephew, was into mystery and magic these days, and had requested a shrunken head, but his parents had vetoed that idea.

Thinking a voodoo doll might be a good substitute, Kerry checked the bottom for the price and was annoyed to see that the doll was made in another country. She put it back.

One of the brochures had mentioned a place that stocked "authentic" voodoo items made by local practitioners. She studied the map the concierge at the hotel had given her that morning. The shop was a block from the museum, which was located on a nearby street in the Quarter.

It wasn't two o'clock yet, so Kerry decided to stroll the sunny streets of the Big Easy, before delving into the darker side of America's most haunted city.

SHORTLY AFTER TWO, Kerry arrived at the voodoo museum. The jawbone of an alligator was mounted over the front door. From her reading, she knew this was a good *Ju-Ju,* meant to ward off evil spirits.

If the thing didn't fall on her head, she would count that as lucky, she decided as she went inside.

Kerry understood at once why the waitress had suggested she come during a quiet hour. The museum was tiny, the bottom floor of an old row house. If she'd met someone in the hall, they would have had to turn sideways to pass.

The pungent aroma of incense tickled her nose. The place was so silent the hair stood up on the back of her neck. A sign indicated a modest fee to see the artifacts, so she began to count out the exact amount.

"Please come in," a low feminine voice said. "I am Queen Patrice, your guide into the other-world."

Kerry nearly dropped the money as every nerve in her body tightened spontaneously.

A woman in a type of gypsy outfit stood in a doorway off the hall. She wore a purple scarf over her head. Sooty black hair spilled from under it and lay in waves down to her waist.

Her eyes were outlined in black with a long line that slanted up to her temples. Bands of purple and gold were brushed over her eyelids, and her full lips were a brilliant carmine.

The blouse she wore matched the scarf and coordinated with a swirling skirt of purple, green and gold, the traditional colors of Mardi Gras. Dangling earrings, sparkling bangles and several necklaces of gold coins completed the outfit. There was nothing threatening about the woman, but Kerry felt slightly uneasy.

"You have arrived at a propitious moment," the woman told her. "Come. I will show you the other rooms."

"Who do I pay?" Kerry asked, indicating the cash clutched in her hand. She made herself relax.

"I'll take it."

In the flick of an eyelash, the money disappeared into a fold in the woman's skirt. With a swishing sound and a rippling wave of purple, green and gold, the voodoo queen led the way into another room.

"Ah, Jolie is awake. Would you like a picture taken with her?"

Kerry's heart did a double back flip when she spied a huge python—no, *two* of them. "A picture?" she echoed.

The woman's eyes narrowed. "It is a great honor."

Kerry knew her nephew would be awed and over-joyed to show off the photo to friends. "Uh, sure. How much does it cost?"

"Nothing. I'll use your camera."

"Oh." Kerry handed over the digital camera, a gift from Ben two Christmases ago. A tiny pang went through her, but she ignored it.

"I'll see if she's willing." The woman opened the cage. "Madame Jolie? I have someone here for you."

Kerry briefly worried that the rest of that statement might be "to eat." The snake looked more than large enough to swallow a person who was five-two and wore a size four petite dress.

"Ah, she's agreed."

Kerry tried to appear nonchalant as Queen Patrice directed her to stand beside the cage. Next, she draped the snake around Kerry's shoulders like a shawl. "Hold her right here," she directed.

Kerry did as told. She and the snake studied each other while the woman circled Kerry's waist with the creature and let its tail end trail over the side of the cage.

"She's, uh, heavy," Kerry commented.

"Naturally. She's full-grown, a queen in her own right."

"I see." Kerry was beginning to have doubts about this photo op.

The docent turned away, but not before Kerry caught a glimpse of a suppressed smile. She inhaled deeply, then smiled as the camera was brought into focus. She wasn't going to act the frightened tourist. Her nephew would never forgive her.

After three poses, the woman returned Jolie to her cage and the camera to Kerry, then departed, leaving Kerry to wander around the crowded rooms until she'd absorbed the information in the displays on voodoo and its history.

Marie Laveau had been the premier queen of voodoo, a woman who'd created her own legend as skillfully as she'd practiced her craft, it seemed.

At a table in the front room, Queen Patrice invited Kerry to join her for tea. "I will tell your fortune. And you must buy *gris-gris* bags for your nephew and nieces before you leave New Orleans."

Kerry gasped. "How did you know about them?"

"The spirits inform me. If they do not, then Madame Jolie does."

Every hair follicle on Kerry's body contracted. Before she could leap from the chair, Queen Patrice laid a hand on hers. "Give me your hand," she said in a very soft voice that nevertheless held a command.

Kerry let the woman turn her palm up and study it for several minutes.

"You are recovering from a sadness," Queen Patrice

said. "But your heart isn't broken, although you may think it is."

Kerry silently scoffed. Fortune-tellers always told their victims some vague tale of woe, then predicted great happiness would soon follow.

"An adventure awaits you. Follow it to the end."

Now for the great happiness part, Kerry thought.

"Perhaps it will lead to sorrow, too," the woman said, her voice going so soft that Kerry had to lean forward to hear the words. "I see a tragedy."

The hair on her neck rose. Sheesh! She must be getting freaked out by this place if she was starting to take this voodoo stuff seriously.

"But you must follow the shining path that begins tonight, Twelfth Night, all the way to the summer solstice or else you'll forever change the course of your history and all who touch your life on this day."

Kerry nodded, the promise wrung out of her by the intense focus of the woman's eyes, which were very dark and shadowed by extremely long false eyelashes.

Queen Patrice released her hand and poured them each a cup of tea. "Drink. It will calm your spirit."

"Thanks." Kerry managed a smile and tried to act like an amused tourist who was taking the performance with a grain of salt. "I think my nephew would like a voodoo doll. Can you recommend one? I'll get the *gris-gris* bags, too. Oh, and charms for my nieces. The girls are into those."

"Yes. I will show you several to choose from."

While Kerry drank the flavored tea, Queen Patrice brought several items to the table. Kerry made her choices and handed over her credit card.

"You must get this for yourself," the woman said. She fastened a charm bracelet around Kerry's wrist. "It is sterling silver. Here. This charm is a cross. It has been blessed with holy water. Use it if you are out at night."

"To ward off vampires?" Kerry asked.

"And werewolves," the queen said, seemingly dead serious. "There are ghosts, too, but they are usually benign, only sad because they were betrayed by those they loved and trusted."

"I know the feeling," Kerry said before thinking.

The docent touched Kerry's arm gently, then withdrew to take care of the payment.

Kerry checked the charms on the bracelet. She found the tiny cross mentioned by Queen Patrice, a group of three bones, a charm shaped like a feather and another like a tiny bag. The *gris-gris*, she assumed.

She hoped these charms brought her good luck while she was here in New Orleans. So far, she'd had nothing but problems. It had been snowing when she'd left Minnesota, her plane had been delayed at takeoff because of the storm, and she'd arrived well after ten last night, worried and tired.

At least the hotel staff had welcomed her warmly.

"Here you go," Queen Patrice said, placing a shopping bag on the table and returning the credit card.

"I boxed and wrapped the items, so they're ready as gifts."

"Thank you. I should get something for my sister, too. Maybe one of these charm bracelets?" she suggested, pointing at her own.

The woman shook her head. "You may see something later that you like better. You should wait."

Kerry nodded. "That's probably a good idea. Well, this has been a very, uh, enlightening afternoon. The museum was fascinating, and thanks again for all your help with my souveniers."

"It was nothing. Wait. I have thought of something." From the pocket hidden in the skirt, she removed a purple ticket and handed it to Kerry. "The old queen will be performing a healing rite tomorrow night. You might like to attend. It is an authentic ceremony. The directions for the location are on the back of the pass."

Kerry stared at the ticket in her hand. She wasn't sure about attending a voodoo ceremony at night, but it seemed rude to refuse outright. Instead she stored it in her wallet and headed out the door. "It was nice talking to you," she said, relieved to be outside in daylight again.

Glancing back, she saw the young voodoo queen standing in the doorway, watching her. In the bright sunlight, Kerry realized the woman's eyes were a deep blue, not black.

A smile warmed the voodoo queen's solemn expression for a second before she turned and closed the door behind her.

Kerry stopped in her tracks. "Oh, for heaven's sake," she muttered, "that was Patti."

Relieved laughter burst from her. For a few minutes she'd actually believed all that hocus-pocus.

Ah, New Orleans. Voodoo queens. Pythons. Vampires. Werewolves. And don't forget the ghosts.

She laughed again. Probably Patti had been putting her on a bit with that voodoo queen act, but it had worked its own kind of magic and Kerry felt less lonely than she had that morning. She would stop by the restaurant tomorrow and tell Patti how much she'd enjoyed the museum—

"Read your fortune, my dear?" A wizened old woman, dressed in black with a black lace mantilla, tried to grab her hand.

Kerry evaded her grasp. "No, thanks. I just had a reading."

Smiling, she ambled along the street. The temperature, in the mid sixties, felt almost balmy compared with Minnesota. She glanced in several shops for a special gift for her sister. Maybe Kerry could find a potion of some kind for both Sharon and her husband—perhaps an aphrodisiac. They might need it after being cooped up with sick children for so long.

Before dark, she found an ideal gift—several small sample bottles of rum and special tins of coffee in a carved wooden box that could be used for jewelry when it was empty. The store would even ship it for her.

She pulled out her credit card and tried not to wince at the total. After all, the rest of the trip was free.

Walking along the park, she took in the sights along the Mississippi River—the Mississippi!—and thought of Mark Twain and his days on the river, of fancy gamblers and even fancier ladies of the evening, and those other queens of the famous city, the steamboats that plied the waters, calliopes blasting.

She watched the *Creole Queen* leave her portage and head up the river. As she lifted her hand against the last rays of the setting sun, the charms on the silver bracelet gleamed and danced before her eyes. They tinkled against each other in the breeze off the river and whispered secrets that hinted at the great adventure that supposedly awaited her.

"Bring it on," she murmured wryly.

KERRY RETURNED to the hotel in the soft, sultry dark. The streets were more crowded than they had been at high noon. A good-looking young man, probably all of twenty, tried to hit on her.

Things were looking up, she decided as she passed him and kept walking. Fingering the charm bracelet and finding the blessed cross, she considered the advice of Queen Patrice. While werewolves didn't hold much appeal for her, she thought a handsome vampire might be just the thing.

"May I kiss you on the neck? May I take a little bite?"

She mentally chuckled, recalling the line from a silly high school play they'd put on as a fund-raiser to buy classroom computers. The tallest, thinnest senior boy had been the vampire. Not exactly the type she had in mind—

"Miss Johnston," the concierge called to her when she entered the Hotel Marchand.

Kerry glanced over to see Luc—oh, yes, Carter, she remembered—approaching her with a smile. He was the one who had welcomed her last night and assured her that a late arrival was no problem.

Like Patti, he was probably in his twenties, late twenties—she decided, since he was the concierge of a grand old hotel, and one didn't get to that position without some prior experience.

With his sandy blond hair, blue eyes and all-American good looks, he could have posed for one of the Mardi Gras posters that showed handsome couples having a great time.

"Here's the list of musical venues you requested," he said, holding out a paper. "I believe there's also a package for you. It was delivered about ten minutes ago."

"For me?" she asked, taking the list from him.

"Yes. I'll check with the bell captain."

Intrigued, she followed Luc to the captain's desk. The man confirmed she did indeed have a package. Kerry's eyes went wide when he lifted a huge basket from beneath the counter. It contained flowers, Mardi Gras trinkets, chocolates, fruit and a bottle of champagne.

"Are you sure that's for me?" she asked.

The bell captain handed her the card with a gallant flourish. "For Miss Kerry Johnston."

The gift was from her sister and brother-in-law. The message told her to enjoy herself "or else!!!" She laughed softly at the threat.

"I'll get someone to carry this for you." He called to a bellhop and indicated the basket. "Miss Johnston needs help to get this to her room, patio suite 2."

"Delighted," the young man answered.

After thanking the concierge and the captain for their help, Kerry followed the bellhop to the French doors that led outside. Like the concierge, the bellhop was young and good-looking, with skin the color of a rich café au lait and golden-brown eyes. She wondered if the hotel hired only sinfully handsome men.

"You have an admirer," he said, carefully carrying the basket to avoid bumping any of the antique tables and lamps as he led the way out to the courtyard and her room.

"A secret one," she murmured, deciding on impulse not to admit the gift came from relatives.

"The very best kind," he declared.

They walked past the pool and the bellhop opened the gate to the private patio garden that fronted the entrance to her quarters. She'd been astounded to discover she was staying in one of the hotel's exclusive units.

"On the table?" the bellhop asked.

"Yes, that would be great." She debated how much she was supposed to tip him, then gave him a five. After all, she was in a luxury patio suite.

"Shall I open the champagne?" he asked. "It's been chilled."

"Uh, not now. Maybe later."

"I'll see that it's iced," he promised and left the room with a brisk stride.

Kerry tossed her purse on the table, sniffed an elegant white lily in the arrangement beside her basket, and wondered what to do next. She suddenly felt hungry, then remembered that she hadn't had dinner yet.

It was almost eight, she realized with a glance at the ornate wall clock. In White Bear Lake, restaurants stopped serving at ten on weeknights and midnight on Saturdays.

But this was New Orleans. Everything probably stayed open all night.

She was too tired to go out again, and she didn't want to go alone in any case. She realized she'd grown complacent about having her fiancé for a companion for four years. Perhaps that had been the basis of their relationship—it was easier to stay together than face being alone.

Chez Remy was the hotel restaurant, but she hadn't been there yet. She glanced down at her casual clothing. It was probably a pretty fancy place.

She spent a few minutes freshening up, then changed

into a long black skirt and pale peach organza blouse with matching camisole. Once she was ready, she headed back out to the courtyard.

Chairs and tables dotted the flagstones, and almost all were occupied. The events rooms glowed with candlelight and music from a live band spilled out into the courtyard. More revelers appeared to have arrived for the Twelfth Night party since she'd retired to her room and prepared for dinner.

The music changed to a fast number. A distinguished-looking man, with gray hair at his temples, caught her hand as she walked by and pulled her to join the couples dancing in the courtyard.

Falling into the spirit of the evening, Kerry let him lead her in a few steps, but when he spun her around, she waved farewell and headed toward the doors leading to the restaurant.

He blew her a kiss and found another partner.

In the restaurant, she was seated at once and had a view of the main lobby. She knew that tickets were required to attend the Twelfth Night Celebration, but she felt sure that by the end of the evening there would be a lot of party crashers there.

At the waiter's suggestion, she started the meal with a shrimp cocktail and tangy red sauce.

On the back of the menu, Kerry read a brief history of the hotel, which covered an entire city block and contained an art gallery as well as the hotel, restaurant, bar and guest rooms. The hotel had been run by Remy

Marchand and his wife, Anne, until Remy's death four years ago.

Kerry knew the Marchand daughters were all involved with the family business. Charlotte Marchand managed the hotel. Kerry had seen her name and title on the confirmation letter for her reservation. Melanie had apparently followed in her father's footsteps and was a chef in the restaurant. Renee Marchand was in charge of public relations, according to the hotel services booklet in her suite, and she was pretty sure the fourth Marchand sister ran the art gallery she'd visited that morning. The hotel was truly a family affair.

The waiter, Henri, a tall, thin man with an aura of regal dignity, returned. He placed a crystal flute of sparkling wine before her.

"From Ms. Charlotte," he explained. "She likes to extend a special welcome to our guests on their first night in the dining room."

"Please thank her for me. If the rest of my visit is as lovely as the first day has been, I'll have many wonderful memories to take home."

When she was alone, she sipped from the flute, smiling as the bubbles tickled her nose. Mmm, after a week of this, she just might get used to living in the lap of luxury. Champagne, two attractive men flirting with her—things were definitely looking up.

However, after dinner, as she wound her way through cluster of people dancing, talking, and laughing in the courtyard, she became somber once more, her own solitude weighing on her spirits.

She unlocked the door and went inside her room. The bedside lamp was on, the covers were turned down, and a china plate with a fruit knife and fork were tucked into a snowy linen napkin beside the gift basket. The champagne nestled in a silver ice bucket as promised, and two crystal flutes stood beside it.

The empty room reminded Kerry she was alone in this very romantic city, which would have made the perfect honeymoon hideaway.

Hot tears filled her eyes and spilled down her cheeks. She sat in a wicker chair, reminiscent of plantations and rum punches, and sobbed her heart out.

After a few minutes, feeling foolish for weeping, Kerry undressed, hung her clothes in the antique wardrobe and pulled on her pajamas.

Over the sounds from the courtyard, she could hear a bell begin to chime the hours, then, without warning, the lights went out.

She stood in the dark for a good two minutes, waiting for the power to come back on.

When it didn't, she sighed. It was becoming harder to convince herself that she was meant to have a good time on this trip. Feeling her way around the room, she found her purse and the pretty box of matches she'd picked up earlier in the day. With the illumination of a match, she managed to get the wick on the hurricane lamp burning. Luckily she knew how to operate this type of lamp. Power outages were common occurrences in her hometown during winter blizzards.

Spotting the champagne, she decided it was time to be daring—do something different in her life. She would soak in the claw-foot tub, using the hotel's Parisian bath oil, until the hot water ran out.

Before she could change her mind, she headed into the bathroom and turned on the spigots full force. Gathering up the silver champagne bucket and flute, she placed them close to the tub, then went back into the bedroom to gather the decorative candles. After opening the champagne and pouring herself a glass, she lit the candles and added the bath oil to the tub. *Perfect.*

Tossing her pajamas aside, she slipped into the frothy water. Now this was living. She lifted the flute to her lips and took a sip. Delicious. She raised the glass again. And again.

A couple of thumps sounded next door. The guest in the adjoining patio suite must have come home. A handsome, witty and unattached male? Perhaps her great adventure, the shining path foretold by Queen Patrice, was about to begin.

Smiling, she refilled the flute and added another inch of hot water to the tub. After tucking a towel behind her neck, she slid down until the water touched her chin.

Ah, bliss…

A sound caused her hand to jerk, and she spilled

several drops of the golden champagne into the water.
She must have drifted off for a while. On the alert now,
she listened intently. The noise was louder this time.

Thump. Thump. A curse followed.

Ah, the next-door neighbor. Hearing the person
stumbling around, Kerry concluded the electricity
must still be off.

The candles were getting low, so she blew them out.
She didn't want to risk falling asleep in the tub again.
Quickly she climbed out and dried off, then pulled on
her pajamas and went to bed. She placed the lamp and
the matches on the side table, turned down the wick
and fell asleep at once.

CHAPTER TWO

JOHN MATHIAS ANDERSON III, called Matt by his family to distinguish him from his grandfather and uncle, nodded to the night clerk as he crossed the lobby of the elegant Hotel Marchand. Candles and lanterns cast a soft light over the elegant lobby, but not to create a romantic mood.

A major power outage had hit the city, or at least this portion of it. The cab driver had assured him the outage was temporary when he'd dropped him in front of the hotel and that all the hotels had generators, but that didn't seem to be the case at the Hotel Marchand.

The lack of electricity obviously hadn't interrupted the Twelfth Night celebration going on in the hotel and spilling into the courtyard. Dancers frolicked in his path as he tried to get to his patio suite.

He edged around the flagstone perimeter, which was dark enough to be spooky, tripped over an urn filled with flowers and got a mouthful of lilies as he muttered a curse.

The pleasure of an evening of wine tasting at a private club, followed by a fine dinner, wasn't diminished by the trek in the dark to his quarters. He closed the patio gate behind him and made his way to the door.

When he inserted the key into the lock, he found the door was ajar. Damn, but he would have to be more careful when he went out. New Orleans had its share of thieves, the same as any city in the country.

He pushed the door closed behind him, then checked the lock. It didn't engage. Flicking the light switch to no avail, he felt around the lock and found the heavy brocade drapes of the window in the way. Holding the material aside, he pushed the door shut and heard the lock click into place.

Yawning hugely, he undressed in the dark, fumbled his way to the bathroom, brushed his teeth and headed for bed.

As he'd expected, the covers were turned back. By feeling around, he located the mint on the pillow, tossed it toward the bedside table and fell into bed.

"What the hell?" he said in a furious bellow.

Someone was in the bed!

He leaped from the mattress, hands raised in self-defense, and stumbled backward against the table. He and a vase hit the carpet. He heard it break.

"Hey, you," he called, standing and peering through the inky blackness when the person didn't say a word.

He cursed again and fumbled around the room until he found the matches he'd seen earlier in a crystal bowl next to a candle in a glass container. Striking a match, he bent over the bed.

A white-faced, black-haired Goldilocks slept peacefully, her arms thrown wide, her hair flowing around her like a dark river. Never in his thirty-seven years had he run into something as bizarre as this.

"Hey, wake up," he said, louder this time.

Someone knocked at the adjoining door between the suites.

"Is everything okay?" a feminine voice called from the other side.

He heaved a sigh. "No, it isn't. There's somebody in my bed. A woman. She's out cold."

"You don't know her?"

Matt glanced at the door in exasperation. "Hardly. I just arrived in town this morning. Ouch!"

He dropped the match as it burned his finger. It flickered out before it hit the carpet. The room went pitch-black again. He, who rarely cursed, muttered a few more choice words. A faint gleam of light appeared at the patio door. A knock followed.

He felt his way around the bed. A woman stood there. She was dressed in a robe of red Chinese silk with cotton pajama legs showing at the bottom.

She stood maybe five-two in her slippers. Her hair spiked out around her head in an impish halo and her eyes looked huge in her heart-shaped face. She carried an old-fashioned oil lamp, which gave off the scent of jasmine as it burned.

"May I help?" she asked.

"I hope so." He ran a hand through his hair. "I think

I didn't shut the door properly when I went out earlier. The curtain gets in the way so the lock doesn't catch. This woman must have been partying pretty hard in the courtyard and stumbled in here to sleep it off." He gestured toward the bed.

She glanced into the room then back at Matt. "I see."

As Matt stepped aside to let her enter, he realized— and so did his guest, he was sure—that he wore nothing but the black briefs he'd left on when he'd undressed. A quick survey of the floor revealed his pants in a heap at the end of the bed. Hurriedly he pulled them on, then joined the woman at the side of the bed.

They both stared at the figure lying there. The white makeup on her face and black kohl outlining her eyes made her look ghostly. Her lipstick was dark, too, like dried blood.

His neighbor took the limp wrist that lay on the coverlet and pressed her fingers against the inside to check the woman's pulse. After a moment, she placed the lamp on the night table and sat on the side of the bed. She felt for a pulse in the woman's neck.

At the anxious expression on her face, Matt felt himself tensing up, too. He had a feeling that the situation wasn't a simple matter of a drunk in his bed.

At last she raised luminous eyes to him. "I think…I think she's… She doesn't seem to be breathing."

"Judas Priest," he said, an expression he hadn't used since college days, some fifteen years ago.

"Well, see if you can find a pulse," she invited rising from the bed with a frown as if he'd disputed her word.

He, too, checked the woman's wrist and then her neck. "My God," he muttered, realizing his neighbor was right.

"Call the police," she said. "I've been trained in CPR. I don't know if it'll help…"

She quickly leaned over the woman in the bed and began treatment.

Matt found the phone and dialed. He got the night clerk first and explained the situation.

"Wait a minute," the clerk said. "I'll get the boss."

Matt waited a couple of minutes before a woman's voice came on the line. She asked him to explain exactly what the problem was. He demanded to know who she was.

"Charlotte Marchand, general manager," she told him. "The night clerk says there's a strange woman in your room?"

"Yes."

"I'll contact the police and be there in a minute. Don't touch anything."

Matt hung up. "The manager's on her way over."

She nodded and began pumping the heart again. "This doesn't seem to be working."

"Is there an obstruction?"

After checking, she shook her head. "Not that I can see." She tried the breathing routine again. There was no lifting of the chest as she tried to force air in.

She rose and shook her head. "We need help." She stood at the end of the bed beside him, her face reflecting the sense of worry and shock that affected them both.

After a few seconds, she said, "I'm Kerry Johnston. From Minnesota."

"I'm Matt Anderson. Glad to meet you." He realized how inane that sounded in view of the circumstances. "New York's my home, but I travel a lot," he added to bridge the awkward moment.

He pulled a T-shirt from a drawer and yanked it over his head, then put on socks and shoes. Now that he was dressed, he felt slightly more in control.

"Have a seat," he suggested to Kerry. "I think it's going to be a long night."

She nodded her thanks when he pulled out a side chair for her. He sat in the matching one while they waited for the manager and the police to arrive.

"Oh, my God," his guest said suddenly, getting to her feet and striding to the bed in two bounds. "I know who she is. I just realized—I know her."

She sounded so distressed that Matt stood, too, and instinctively placed his arm around her narrow shoulders.

"Who is she?" he asked.

"Patti. Dear God, it's Patti. She was my waitress at lunch today. And the docent at the voodoo museum."

Matt's scalp prickled. "I was at one of the voodoo museums this afternoon." He studied the still face on his pillow. "She could have been the clerk who sold me a book on the history of voodoo in New Orleans for my mother—"

A knock at the patio door interrupted them.

Matt went to open it. A woman stood there, holding a battery-powered lantern.

"Charlotte Marchand?" he asked. Like Kerry, this woman was petite, with auburn hair and almond-shaped green eyes.

"Yes."

"Matt Anderson," he introduced himself. "Kerry…"

"Johnston," she supplied.

"What happened?" Charlotte wanted to know, going to the bed and bending over the figure.

She held her lantern close to the gaudily painted face on the pillow. Charlotte checked the pulse as Kerry had done. *"Mon Dieu,"* she muttered. "She *is* dead."

"I tried CPR, but it didn't seem to help," Kerry told her. "Her lungs won't inflate."

Matt felt a complete sense of unreality. "Have you called the police?"

"Security is taking care of it, but the police are overtaxed with the blackout. I wanted to make sure this wasn't some kind of joke."

"A joke," Kerry echoed in disbelief.

"It's the beginning of Mardi Gras," the manager said as if this explained everything. She removed a cell phone from her waist and punched in a number. After a short conversation, she turned back to them.

"Security was alerted when I was. The police and an ambulance should be here as soon as possible. You'll have to stay until the police arrive, then we can move you to another room."

"Miss Johnston is next door," Matt explained. "She heard me stumble into the table when I discovered there was another person in my bed and came over to help."

This whole situation was like a scene out of some diabolical play. And he didn't know his part. Neither did Kerry. He was sorry he'd involved her in the awful incident.

"When I dialed 9-1-1," he continued, anger now invading his voice, "I got the front desk."

"You must not have dialed 9 to get an outside line," the manager explained.

A man appeared at the door of the suite. "Tyrell said there was a problem." His gaze took in the dead woman and the room in one sweeping glance.

Charlotte explained all they knew.

"You don't know who she is?" the man asked Matt.

"Who are you?" Matt demanded.

"He's head of security here," Charlotte told him. "Mac Jensen. This is Mr. Anderson's room, Mac. He doesn't know how the...this person came to be in here."

Matt spoke to the security guy. "I realized when I came in tonight that the lock doesn't engage because the curtain gets in the way. It's too close to the door."

"I'll have that taken care of. Right now we have to keep everything the same for the police," Charlotte said grimly. "This is all we need—a death in addition to the power outage and the generator not working—"

She stopped abruptly as if she'd given too much away.

Matt felt rather sorry for the manager and her team, who would have to deal with the repercussions of the tragedy.

The security chief checked for a pulse. Kerry told him about administering CPR and said there seemed to be a blockage in the airway. He glanced toward the courtyard. "I think we'd better tell the band to bring the evening to a close." He glanced at the manager.

"Would you do that?" she requested. "That would be one less thing to worry about."

"Unless someone in the crowd is involved in this." Matt waved a hand toward the bed.

They stared at the still form.

"I don't see any signs of struggle," Jensen said. "No blood or bruising on her." He glanced around the room again and frowned. "The vase is broken—"

"I did that," Matt admitted. "I jumped from the bed when I realized there was someone else here."

"Could it be an overdose?" Charlotte said to the security man. "You know there are people on the street selling everything one can imagine."

Matt observed the manner in which the security

chief checked the room and relaxed a bit. The man was sharp-eyed and intelligent, his mind focused.

"Anyone connected with the victim would have fled long ago," Jensen said. "I'll go out front and direct the cops in here. They can decide if we should send the partygoers home and call it a night."

When he left, the silence stretched to the four corners of the room.

"This is most unfortunate," Charlotte said to Matt and Kerry. "I'm so sorry you've been pulled into such a bad situation."

Matt shrugged. "That's life," he said, trying not to be judgmental and accuse her and the staff of not doing their jobs properly. He thought about changing hotels. With a glance at Kerry's pale face, he wondered if she would like to move, too.

Charlotte nodded and managed a grim smile. "A guest has left unexpectedly, so there's another patio suite available, number three, on the other side of Miss Johnston's. We'll move you there after the police give their approval."

Kerry gave him a smile as if urging him to accept.

He nodded, then wondered why she should have any influence on his decisions.

Because she'd come when he'd needed her.

That was an odd thought. At thirty-seven, he'd made it a rule to never let himself rely on anyone else for emotional or financial support. He'd worked through high school and college to support himself, separating himself from his father in all the ways he could. If it weren't for his mother, he doubted he'd ever bother to speak to the man.

But that was the past.

After writing for the college paper, he'd chosen journalism as his field, rather than the law profession, as his father and grandfather had demanded. Youthful defiance maybe, but he'd worked his way into a career he enjoyed—wine critic for a slick and expensive magazine headquartered in New York.

He traveled the world looking for the best wines and restaurants with the best-stocked cellars. He'd written three books, all still in print, one of them a nonfiction bestseller on living the good life.

He'd worked his butt off to show his family he had chosen the *best* life for him.

"Did anyone check for identification on the body?" Jensen asked.

"Patti." Kerry suddenly spoke up. "Her name is Patti. I met her earlier today. At the voodoo museum, she called herself Queen Patrice, but she was Patti, the waitress, at the restaurant where I had lunch."

Charlotte looked weary as she took in this information. Matt guessed she'd had a stressful night.

"All the women who practice voodoo call themselves queens," she said. "It comes from Marie Laveau's tomb. It says she was a voodoo queen, so every claimant calls herself one, too."

Matt noted how her gaze took in the details of the

room, as if she were searching for clues to what had happened earlier. In addition to the broken vase, which he'd knocked on the floor, the room had a disheveled appearance.

Clothing hung out of the lower drawers of the armoire as if someone had rifled through them. The notepad and pen beside the phone were askew, as if hurriedly pushed aside.

He was positive he hadn't disturbed the room in that manner. Had the young woman...Patti, he corrected, glancing at Kerry, who now looked sad and drawn. Had Patti gone through his things, maybe looking for money for another drug hit?

"Kerry had nothing to do with this," he said. "Can't she go to her room? The police can get a statement from her tomorrow if they need it."

"She'd better stay," Charlotte told him, giving Kerry a sympathetic glance.

The security chief appeared at the door at that instant. "The police," he announced and led two men inside. He introduced them as detectives from homicide. "Crime scene investigators."

Charlotte moved away from the bed. "I'm not sure there's been a crime. It may be an overdose."

"We'll check it out," the older of the two men said. "Who found the body?"

"I did," Matt said. "She was in my room when I came in. The electricity was off and I undressed in the dark, then went to bed. That's when I discovered her—Patti."

Both officers gave him a sharp glance. "You know her?" the older one asked.

"No," he said.

"I did," Kerry told them. "I met her today. She was my waitress at lunch." She told them where. The younger detective wrote the info down. "Then she was the docent at the voodoo museum this afternoon, only she called herself Queen Patrice. She took my picture with Jolie—the python," she added at the blank expressions on the men's faces.

Matt reassessed Kerry's delicate frame. If she'd agreed to have her picture taken with a snake as large as a python, she must be stronger than she looked.

And braver.

He liked the way she'd come over to help him out when he'd discovered a strange woman in his bed. That showed a level of confidence that he admired.

Independent women appealed to him. Kerry wasn't at all like the women in his family. For years, he'd wondered why his mom didn't leave his father, a ruthless, controlling man. Finally he'd realized she couldn't, that she didn't know how to live her life without someone like her husband to take charge.

Or maybe she was willing to put up with the cold temper and authoritative ways in order to live a comfortable life as the wife of a successful lawyer and community leader.

He sighed and wondered what had brought about

these ruminations. Glancing at Kerry, who waited patiently beside him for the police to finish, he had an odd impulse to take her hand and kiss it to thank her for coming over, for being cool and levelheaded when confronted with such a difficult situation.

She looked over at him and gave him a wan smile that spoke of weariness and empathy.

After the detectives had gotten a statement from everyone, paramedics arrived with a gurney and quietly took the body of Patti, alias Queen Patrice, from the room.

Once the police and paramedics were gone, Charlotte and Matt walked Kerry to her door and bid her good-night, then continued to the next suite.

Charlotte unlocked the door with a master key. "I'll have a bellboy pack for you and bring you a key to this suite."

"Fine," Matt said.

"Thank you so much for your patience." Charlotte shook his hand. "I can't tell you how much I regret what has happened."

He shrugged. "It was a shock, but things happen that are beyond anyone's control."

"I hope you rest well," she said. She departed, leaving a battery-powered lantern for him.

Next door, he heard a slight noise and wondered if his neighbor would be able to sleep.

Glancing at the elegant bed in his new quarters,

he gave a rueful sigh, then secured the interior bolt and chain.

One ghastly surprise per night was more than enough for Matt.

CHAPTER THREE

THE SUN WAS HIGH and the temperature in the sixties by the time Kerry emerged from her room on Sunday morning. Dressed in white slacks and a long-sleeved, green silky blouse, she crossed the courtyard on the way to Chez Remy.

Attempting to join in the spirit of the Mardi Gras season, she wore two earrings with dangling stars in her left earlobe and one earring, a smiling moon, in the other. This was good *Ju-Ju*, according to the street vendor who'd sold them to her. Between those and the charm bracelet, she should be safe from the city's otherworldly elements. And shocks such as the one last night, she thought.

"Kerry, good morning," a deep voice said.

Matt Anderson sat at an outside table. A waiter placed an insulated pitcher of coffee near his cup. The power had come on sometime in the night, and the staff must have worked overtime, because the hotel felt surprisingly back to normal.

"Join me?" he invited.

Kerry nodded. Matt stood and held a chair for her.

"I'm having the cold breakfast buffet, but there are hot items like eggs, bacon and grits if you want the full service."

"Cereal and fruit is my usual, so I'll have the cold buffet, too," she told the waiter. "And coffee, please."

The man flipped her napkin open, laid it across her lap, then filled a coffee cup for her. He departed, only to return in less than a minute with pitchers of water and orange juice. He filled the stemmed goblets already in place on the natural grass mats, then left Matt and Kerry.

"Did you sleep at all?" Matt asked, his deep-set eyes as solemn as a surgeon's.

Kerry was taken aback as she gazed into eyes the color of the blue-eyed Marys that grew on her grand-parents' farm back home. His hair was blond with darker undertones, like fields of ripe wheat, and had a stubborn wave that the short, stylish haircut couldn't quite subdue.

When he'd held the chair for her, she'd realized he was quite tall, probably six feet.

Last night, with all that had been going on, she'd been much too upset to notice just how impressive he was in the looks department. As if to belie the thought, a distinct memory of a toned body in black briefs with long, muscular legs flashed across her mind. With an effort, she forced it aside.

"Yes, actually I did." She managed a smile. "It sur-prised me that I woke so late, even with all that happened. I'm always up by seven at home, even on the days I don't have to get to work."

"What kind of work do you do?" Matt asked.

"Dental hygiene. I work in a clinic with four dentists and one other hygienist."

"Do you like your work?"

"Very much. I get to do the good stuff for our patients. No drilling. No root canals. No tightening up braces until the patient feels like screaming."

He returned her grin as she described the tortures of dentistry. "You've made me recall why I hated going to the dentist as a kid—braces."

"Yes, but now you have a perfect smile."

"So the pain was worth it," he concluded. He raised his juice glass in a toast to her. "So do you," he said. "Here's to the good neighbor who came to my rescue last night."

His expression became serious and he gave a sigh that she thought he was unaware of. She suppressed the need to reach out and touch him in sympathy. Death wasn't something either of them could shake off easily.

At that moment, a man and woman crossed the courtyard, each pulling luggage behind them. "We'll sue," the man muttered to his companion. "We'll get back every penny we've spent on this vacation and then some. Bunch of thieves."

Kerry felt very sorry for whoever was working the registration desk and had to handle the couple and their complaints. There was total silence in their wake, then the other diners began talking again, but in lower tones.

She overheard a man say his room looked as if it had been ransacked. Nothing was missing, his wife reported, but she'd heard things were taken from other rooms.

Matt gave her a troubled glance, "Sounds as if a lot of bad stuff happened last night."

Oblivious to human problems, a fat bee droned by, then circled Kerry's head. She sat perfectly still, then smiled as it landed on a fresh lily in the delicate porcelain vase on the table. It snuggled in the trumpet for a minute, then emerged heavy with pollen.

She and Matt chuckled together as it flew off in a rather precarious manner, as if drunk with nectar.

Matt studied her in a way that made her feel warm and maybe a little uneasy. She envisioned those long legs, the black briefs…

Then she remembered why she'd been in his room and her thoughts sobered.

"Kerry," he said. When she glanced up, he asked, "What made you sigh?"

"Patti," she murmured. "It's so odd to think that a person I was talking to yesterday is…gone. She was so nice, so full of life. Although I think she was putting me on a bit with her voodoo routine and taking my picture with the python." She paused and considered. "But it was odd that she knew things about me, things I know I didn't tell her."

"Such as?"

"Well, she knew I had one nephew and two nieces. She suggested gifts for them. And this charm bracelet for me."

When she laid her arm on the table so he could see, he placed his large, warm hand over hers and studied each charm. "Bones, a *gris-gris* bag, a cross—" he began to recite.

"She said it had been blessed with holy water and would protect me from vampires and werewolves," Kerry told him. "I didn't realize the city had werewolves as well as vampires and ghosts."

"I think the vampires came from some popular novels. I'm not sure about the werewolves. Voodoo, as a religion, pays homage to various spirits, such as the Earth, the Forest, Wisdom, Healing, those kinds of things. It originated in the Benin region of Africa hundreds of years ago, according to the book I bought."

"Then it was transported here with the slave trade?"

"Right." He pointed to the camera tucked into a pocket of her purse. "You said Patti took your picture with a python. Did she use your camera?"

"Yes."

"Is it a digital? Do you have pictures of your family on it?"

"Why, yes. From Christmas." She retrieved the camera and clicked back from the three photos of her and Queen Jolie. "Here's one of my sister, her husband and their kids." She held the camera out for him to see.

"You and your sister favor each other," he said.

"Yes. That's probably how she figured out the one nephew and two nieces. That info almost made me believe she really could read palms." Kerry remembered the voodoo ceremony that night. "That reminds me, Patti gave me a ticket to a ceremony to be performed tonight by an 'old voodoo queen.' At least that's what she said." Kerry found the ticket in her purse and read the information to Matt. "I wonder if I should go."

Matt frowned.

"What is it?" she asked.

"The woman at the voodoo museum I visited gave me one, too. When I got the book for my mother."

"Was she dressed in a purple blouse with a matching scarf and a skirt of purple, gold and green? She had really long false eyelashes and bands of purple and gold shadow on her eyelids."

"I don't remember the colors, but those eyelashes were incredible. I couldn't figure out how she held her eyes open."

A chill ran along every nerve in Kerry's body as Queen Patrice's words reverberated through her.

...follow the shining path that begins tonight, Twelfth Night, all the way to the summer solstice or else you'll forever change the course of your history and all who touch your life on this day.

"Are you going?" she asked Matt.

He shrugged. "I have a tasting this afternoon."

Kerry wondered what that meant.

"Sorry," he said as if reading her mind. "I write articles on all phases of the wine industry from growing the grapes to serving the finished product. I'm covering New Orleans for a feature article on wine clubs and famous cellars in the area."

"Sounds interesting," she said sincerely. "If you don't mind my asking, how did you get into the field?"

"A friend who was dating the managing editor of *Wines of the World* magazine suggested me for a big spread they wanted to do on New York wines. Since my family has interests in a vineyard and winery there, it was a natural fit. Besides working at the vineyard in the summer, I helped my mother put on a charity auction featuring premium wines each year."

"I see."

"Once the article came out, I received an award from a New York wine growers' association for my work. After that, I was a 'known' expert and a lot of assignments came my way. I liked the independence of being a freelance writer, so I quit my newspaper job and focused on writing about wines. Lucky for me, the timing worked out. Wines are just becoming hot."

"To take a chance like that would require more courage than I have." Kerry confessed.

"I don't know about that," Matt teased her. "It takes a lot of courage to have your picture taken with a python and come to the aid of a stranger during a blackout." He smiled at her. "Shall we help ourselves to the buffet?"

They were mostly silent as they ate. Kerry noticed a

family heading for the registration desk with their bags and wondered if a lot of the guests were checking out. The blackout had been disturbing, even without the death.

She glanced at Matt and realized she was drawn to him, not only because of their shared experience, but in other ways, too.

There was more to him than good looks, she realized. He seemed thoughtful, with a candidness that she liked. He'd taken a chance and gone out on his own, making a success of his career. That had taken confidence and courage, and lots of hard work.

Over fresh cups of coffee and warm beignets from the buffet, they spoke of Patti again.

"I wonder who she really was," Kerry said. "The friendly waitress, the voodoo queen, the punk or ghost or whatever she was supposed to be last night."

"After finally going to bed I couldn't sleep," Matt said grimly. "Every time I closed my eyes I saw that white face and the black eyes. She looked ghastly, in my opinion."

"She was really quite lovely, one of the most beautiful women I've ever seen. Really," she added at his skeptical frown. "She looked like a movie star."

"I called the detective this morning," Matt told her.

"One of the two who came last night? I didn't think of that. I was curious about her and wondered if they'd discovered the cause of death. What did he say? Did they contact her family?"

Matt shook his head. "She wrote that she had no next-of-kin on the employment forms she filled out for the restaurant."

"Oh. What about the museum?"

"The detective didn't mention it."

Kerry blinked the sting of tears from her eyes. "She was so nice to me. She seemed to know I was alone and lonely." Her voice sounded shaky, but she hurried on, "Anyway, she sort of took me under her wing and advised me on what to do in the city. I guess she recognized a small-town gal when she saw one." Kerry managed a brief laugh at the description.

"A Florence Nightingale," Matt corrected softly. "That's what I thought of last night when you came to my door, lantern in hand. I was grateful for your offer of help. I didn't realize the seriousness of the situation at the moment. I thought the woman had passed out."

"It's difficult to get over the shock of a death like that," she murmured, "even when it's someone you don't really know. But if she has no family, what will happen to her?"

"The detective said the medical examiner would have to perform an autopsy to discover the cause of death. My guess is she overdosed on something. She may have gotten hold of a bad mix. Then…I don't know…I suppose they have public cemeteries for cases like this."

"That's so sad, not to have anyone who cares if you live or die."

His hand touched hers again. "Don't cry," he said in a tone that flowed around her like a gentle breeze and nearly made her lose it.

She managed to keep the tears at bay. "It's just that I had this cousin who…" Kerry had to stop and swallow. She sucked in a harsh breath. "She committed suicide."

He looked concerned. "When did this happen?"

"Three years ago. The terrible thing was that I'd seen her that morning and asked if things were okay. She said they were, and I believed her. Then she rowed out to the middle of the lake and jumped in. She was a good swimmer but she drowned anyway. The water was icy cold and her clothing weighed her down."

"My God," he said softly. "I'm sorry."

"I've never understood it. We were best friends. How could a person go off without a word to anyone and do that?" She stared at him in entreaty, as if he could explain it so she would understand and the aching hurt would go away.

"I don't know." He hesitated, then added, "I think your situation was worse than what happened to my sister. At least my family knew how she died and that it wasn't her intention."

"Oh, Matt, I'm so sorry for making you remember something terrible in your life."

"It's been sixteen years," he said. "I was twenty-one, a senior in college. She was in Africa with a charity group. A rare virus broke out in the area where they were working, but before the doctors could identify and control it, fifty villagers and five volunteers were dead."

Kerry felt his pain in spite of the calm way he reported the facts and the time that had passed since the tragedy.

"There was a civil war going on. It took weeks to find out that she died, and months to retrieve her body. That was hard on my mother. When we finally had the burial in our family graveyard, it gave us closure."

"But it still hurt," Kerry said softly.

"Yes, it still hurt."

They fell silent, staring into each other's eyes, and Kerry realized that they were holding hands, their fingers tightly clasped as if each saw the other as a lifeline in a world of sadness and grief.

"Fresh coffee?" a familiar voice inquired.

The tension of the moment broke, and she withdrew her hand from Matt's.

"Henri," Kerry said, glad for the diversion. She was slightly unnerved by the deep connection she'd felt with Matt. "Do you work day and night?"

He chuckled, a rich joyful sound that seemed to offset the unease she'd experienced, and shook his head. "I've been here long enough that I can choose my own schedule. I like working a couple of hours during lunch, then four or five hours in the evening. That way, I have my afternoons free for gardening, which is my hobby and my obsession, according to my wife."

Kerry realized it was after eleven. She and Matt had talked well over an hour.

After Henri left them with a fresh pot of coffee, she absently ran her finger around the rim of her cup while she thought of the afternoon ahead.

"What are you going to do today?" Matt asked.

"I don't know." She glanced down at her purse. "One thing I know. I'm going to the ceremony tonight. The ticket describes it as a tribute to the Spirit of Healing. I think I could use some help in that department. My spirits are pretty low at the moment."

Matt nodded. "I know the feeling." He shook his head slightly. "But I'm not sure it's such a good idea for us to attend some voodoo rite."

"Why?"

"Just a gut feeling," he admitted with a self-deprecating grimace. "Maybe we've been through enough. Last night was one hell of an experience."

Kerry couldn't deny that. "When the blackout happened, I thought it was romantic. I was soaking in the bathtub with candles all around, sipping champagne like some decadent, pampered princess. That illusion was soon dispelled."

He leaned forward in an earnest manner. "I'm sorry I spoiled your night and pulled you into my problems."

She assumed a lighter tone. "Hey, what are friends—or neighbors—for? You're right. It was a strange night."

She considered a moment, "I still would like to go to the ceremony. It sounds interesting."

His eyes were on her, his expression thoughtful. "Tell you what—since we both have tickets, let's go together. I should be finished with the wine tasting and back here by six. Shall we have dinner first?"

She nodded, trying hard to ignore the little flutter of anticipation at the thought of spending an evening with Matt.

FOR THE FIRST TIME in a long time, Matt had trouble following the conversation about the excellence of the various wines at this very exclusive wine club, made up of a dozen of the city's oldest, most prominent families. The wine purchaser was a senior member of the group, which had been founded by their ancestors five generations ago.

Roots.

To Matt, they meant obligations and expectations that had nothing to do with his own talents or wishes.

Across the dark walnut table, a young man stared into his wine goblet, then poured the excellent vintage down his throat without bothering with the niceties of aroma, palette and finish. Their host, Claude Pichante, glared at him.

Matt sorted through the earlier introductions. The young man was Jason Pichante. The tasting was taking place in the Pichante home, an elegant mansion in the

Garden District, which fortunately had seen only light damage in the flooding after Hurricane Katrina.

Angry father. Resentful son.

Now where had he seen a similar scenario played out? he asked himself facetiously. His sympathy went at once to the son, but he admitted he could be mistaken.

For some reason, he thought of Kerry. There seemed to be no anger in her, just goodwill and warmth. She was talkative, until the shock of Patti Ruoui's death—the detective had told Matt the dead woman's name—reasserted itself, then those luminous eyes dimmed with sorrow and she fell silent. It obviously bothered her that Patti had no one to mourn her passing, and the death seemed to remind Kerry of her cousin's suicide.

Odd, but whenever Kerry seemed sad, he found he wanted to hold her until the brightness returned to her face.

"A blend of blackberries with a finish of vanilla," Claude Pichante was saying.

Matt forced his mind to attention. He ate a plain cracker to clear his palate, then took a tiny sip from the fresh goblet the white-coated waiter handed him.

He inhaled slowly, letting the flavors flow over and under his tongue. This gave him a clear assessment of the wine's present veracity and its future promise.

"Matt, your thoughts," Pichante said.

"Blackberry and vanilla, yes." Matt agreed with the

host's assessment. "A little strong on the tannin, but balance should be restored by aging. Five years, and this wine will be excellent."

"Ah, my thoughts exactly," the older Pichante said.

Across the table, his son gave a soft, but audible snort. Again he downed the wine.

"Jason, if you have an appointment, you may leave us," his father said, steel undercoating every word.

The other five club members, all elderly gentlemen, continued with the tasting as if they hadn't heard a word.

Matt did the same.

He checked the clock over the mantel. It was nearly time to leave. He was looking forward to dinner with Kerry. As for the healing ceremony, he wasn't so sure.

Jason Pichante suddenly stood up, slammed the exquisitely carved chair backward against the elaborate sideboard and left the room.

Claude sighed. "Children," he murmured. "Jason thinks he's in love. The young woman's most unsuitable, as his mother and I have pointed out."

The guests, Matt included, chuckled over the father-son dilemma, but Matt's sympathies sided more firmly with the son. He could remember more than one society deb being paraded before him as marriage material. At the time, he would have scorned the goddess of love herself if his family had brought her to the house for a weekend gathering.

Not that he'd done so great on his own. Working in

New York City, he'd met a buyer for an expensive boutique and fallen hard. When she found out he mostly avoided his family and they wouldn't be spending weekends and holidays at the upstate family compound surrounded by rich relatives and friends, she'd dropped him for a shipping heir from East Hampton.

After that experience, he'd learned to avoid any mention of his connection to the well-known Andersons. His family's law firm handled contracts for film and music celebrities, and some women had wanted to use him as a springboard for their own careers. He could handle that as long as they were up front about it. Most weren't.

For a second, he wondered what his high-society family would think of a small-town dental hygienist. Kerry was obviously close to her family and had a tender heart where others were concerned. Or so it seemed. He'd been fooled once before by a sweet act that covered a calculating nature. He was doubly on guard now.

Hearing a door slam in another part of the grand mansion, he felt glad to no longer be twenty-something and defiant as only the young can be.

When the tasting was over and Matt had checked his notes against the wine labels to make sure he had the information correct, he thanked his host and assured the group that he was quite impressed with their cellar and the care they took in stocking it.

In fact, it was one of the best tastings he'd had in the city, so he was telling the truth.

With a lighter step, he hailed a taxi and returned to the hotel. In his room, he changed from the blue summer suit to jeans and a long-sleeved shirt. A crewneck sweater would take care of the cooler evening air, he decided, and looped it over his shoulders.

Wallet. The ticket. Yep, he was ready, and it was nearly seven. Time for dinner. He had a place in mind.

Pausing, he wondered if he should knock on the adjoining door. Somehow that felt presumptuous, so instead, he went outside and crossed the patio to her door. He knocked softly.

"Be there in a sec," she called.

When Kerry opened the door, he caught his breath. Like him, she wore jeans and sneakers, with a green knit top that hugged her torso, showing off every curve. She carried a light jacket.

Her eyes reminded him of gemstones, but he couldn't decide which kind. They weren't emerald or peridot, but some enticing blend all their own. Just as the finest wines combined complexity and depth—

"Ready?" she asked, looking up at him expectantly.

He nodded, struck speechless like some kid on a first date.

What the hell was that about? he asked himself, but no answer was forthcoming. "I have a recommendation for a restaurant near here. Shall we go there for dinner?"

She glanced at their clothing. "It isn't formal, is it?"

"No, it's very casual—Cajun cooking. I have the

names of the hottest dishes they serve. I was told no one could claim to know New Orleans cuisine without trying the real stuff."

When she laughed, he did, too. They strolled out into the pleasant twilight.

"Oh," she said, stopping in the courtyard. "Detective Rothberg came by this afternoon. Patti's name is Ruoui. He said the restaurant staff confirmed that she had no immediate family, but she did have a boyfriend. No one knew his name. Apparently she wasn't on intimate terms with any of the other workers."

"Yeah, that's what he said when I talked to him."

"Why didn't you tell me this morning?" she asked, giving him a curious glance.

"Talking about it makes you look so sad," he said simply and took her hand as a crowd of college kids surged by them like a school of dolphin riding out a squall on the ocean.

At her somber expression, he squeezed her hand and, in amused tones, began to tell her about the wine tasting that afternoon. He related the father-son incident to the tension between him and his father while he was growing up.

"An alpha father and alpha son do have a hard time," she told him, gazing up at him in such an earnest manner that he was seized with the urge to kiss her.

He tried to figure out what it was about her that made him feel so impulsive. It was a totally new experience for him.

They had reached the restaurant and in a few minutes were seated at a small round table.

"I can't imagine not getting along with my family," Kerry confided, picking up the conversation where they'd left off. "We're always visiting or calling each other. Not that we have anything important to say. I suppose we just like the sound of our own voices."

Her quiet laughter and the affection in her tone made him envious. "Do you have more than one sister, or any brothers?"

"No, but my mom was from a family of five kids, my dad from three, so there were always lots of cousins around when I was growing up. And lots of adults to keep us in line, lovingly, of course."

"Of course," he said, a picture of the perfect family forming in his mind. Life wasn't like that, but something about this woman conjured up visions of all the good things a person could wish for.

A warmth swept through him as he listened to the lilt in her voice. He was attracted to her, he realized, very attracted.

Last night, after he'd gone to bed—for the second time and in a different suite—he'd thought about her and the red silk robe, the pajama legs visible beneath it, terry scuffs on her feet. She'd been an alluring combination of elegance and practicality.

The women he knew would have been dressed in a matching gown and peignoir set or designer pajamas.

"Beer?" the waiter asked. Before they could answer, he rattled off about twenty microbrews on tap.

Matt shook his head. "I've had my quota of alcohol, but you go ahead if you like," he told Kerry.

"I'll take iced tea," she said.

He ordered the same.

"When you said you were a wine expert, I wondered how you handled all the drinking. My great-uncle was an alcoholic. My family used him as an example of what could happen with excessive alcohol use."

"If you're rich enough, people ignore your drinking," he said, his voice thick with cynicism. "Or cover for you."

Her eyes went wide and solemn, and Matt saw the questions she was too polite to ask.

He found himself answering them. "My family is wealthy. Old money. Long history in the community. Embarrassing incidents have a way of disappearing from the record. Youthful indiscretions are ignored. It also doesn't hurt if the family has a very influential law firm."

"I don't know about altering records," Kerry said, "but being related to lawyers can come in handy. My mom's oldest brother is an attorney. He was thrilled when his son and a nephew decided to study law and went into the firm with him."

"In our family," Matt reported grimly, "the men are expected to enter law." He shrugged. "I chose differently."

"Why?"

Coming from Kerry, the question didn't feel intrusive. Matt knew she was genuinely interested in him as a person. "Probably defiance, the same as Jason Pichante. The high school counselor advised that I had wide-ranging interests and an aptitude for stringing words together. Journalism was one of the fields she suggested I should consider."

"And so you did. A wise decision." Kerry smiled in approval. "You obviously love what you do."

He shrugged. "I make a comfortable living at it."

She beamed at him. "That's the way I feel about my work. I'm lucky to be paid for something I enjoy doing."

It felt like a bond between them. For reasons he couldn't name, Matt liked that idea. He liked it a lot.

CHAPTER FOUR

"MY TONGUE is still burning," Kerry told Matt.

"Mine, too. Cajun cuisine must be an acquired taste."

His rumble of laughter warmed Kerry. She knew he was probably used to much more sophisticated women than a small-town Midwesterner like herself. But at least they could enjoy each other's company.

"Well, I for one am not going to acquire a taste for that rice sausage dish," she declared. "It was so hot I couldn't breathe for a couple of minutes after the first bite. But the filé gumbo was delicious."

"I agree."

They were taking a cab to the voodoo ceremony, and Kerry shivered slightly as they passed a cemetery. She hoped the rite wasn't performed there.

The cabbie let them out at a gate just beyond the graveyard and nodded toward a grove of trees. Lights twinkled between the branches. "Over there," he said, nodding in that direction. "Stay with the crowd and you'll be fine."

Matt paid the man and thanked him. "You will be back to pick us up?"

"Sure thing, mon. Two hours." He handed over a card. "But call if it ends before then."

The driver seemed certain the ceremony would take the full two hours. Kerry glanced toward the cemetery and another shiver pressed along her spine. A wrought-iron fence separated the cemetery from the grove of trees, which was reassuring.

She almost laughed at herself. As if that spindly little fence could keep out ghosts.

When had she started to believe in the supernatural? she wondered. Glancing at her tall handsome companion as they hurried along the path to the edge of the bayou, she was grateful not to be alone.

A slow drumbeat beckoned the followers to gather for the ceremony. Healing, Kerry had learned, also involved cleansing. It was necessary to get rid of the evil in one's heart so that the Spirit of Healing could enter.

As she and Matt walked out of the trees into the clearing, the beat of the drum picked up, becoming softer but more urgent.

"Come," a woman said as if she'd been expecting them for some time. "Sit here."

Kerry tucked her hand into the crook of Matt's elbow and held on, unnerved by the woman's appearance.

Her hair was pure white and very long, past her waist, and spilled from a gold scarf tied gypsy-fashion over her head. Her brown face looked like crumpled paper, it was so lined.

Her makeup was similar to what Patti had worn in her Queen Patrice persona, with gold the dominant color, then green and purple. The woman's blouse and long skirt were black, and she wore a gold-and-green striped cape tied with a purple cord.

"Thank you," Matt said to the crone.

He and Kerry sat where she indicated on a woven grass rug. The man at Matt's left leaned close. "That was the old queen," he said in awe. "You must be special for her to recognize you."

Matt couldn't imagine why. "Have you been to these ceremonies before?"

"Several times. My grandmother lives near here and my family visits every January."

"Is there anything special we're expected to do during the, uh, performance?"

"No. The queen and her court do everything. Every spirit has its song, dance and rhythm. The audience must never do anything to disrupt the flow or the spirit may be displeased and bring disaster to us all."

"I hope we're doing the right thing by being here," Matt said wryly.

"This is good *Ju-Ju*," the man confided. "The Healing Spirit is gentle. The Earth Spirit requires a blood sacrifice, which bothers some people."

The lonely beat of a single drum suddenly echoed around the clearing and over the opaque waters of the bayou, making it seem as if there were hundreds of drummers.

"The Spirit of Healing," the man told them, "is symbolized by thunder. We'll hear lots of drums tonight. The dancing will be entertaining, and sensuous." He grinned, not in a lewd manner but as one tourist to another.

Matt and Kerry nodded together. Their eyes met. Kerry squeezed Matt's arm, which she hadn't realized she was holding, then let go. He smiled as if assuring her all would be well.

She hoped he was right. Little flashes of nervous tension were racing to all points of her body. If someone said "Boo!" at that moment she would probably have heart failure on the spot.

A young woman, also a voodoo queen judging by her clothing, moved through the group collecting the colored tickets. Matt and Kerry handed her their purple ones. She paused, quickly perused them, then turned the tickets over.

Kerry noticed there were identical markings on the back, a tiny sign like a hand with three fingers raised. She touched her bracelet and found the charm of three bones. For some reason, the symbol seemed comforting.

The voodoo queen gave them a solemn smile and nodded as if in welcome. Her gaze flicked over them again before she continued to the man beside Matt.

Kerry let out a relieved breath, feeling she'd just passed some test.

"Whew," Matt said *sotto voce*, evidently feeling the same. "This is going to be a very interesting evening."

The drums stopped, and the ensuing silence was so profound it was nerve-racking. Even the breeze held its breath.

The old queen walked into the center of the clearing and paced around a fire pit, her eyes on the people seated around her in a circle. Some must be actual practitioners of the voodoo art, Kerry decided as they nodded to the woman.

With a sudden swoop, the old woman bent over the fire pit. Flames, several feet high, leapt skyward from the logs.

A collective "ohh" went up from the onlookers.

The flames settled into a steady pattern, then danced as the breeze picked up again.

The lone drum started its beat. Kerry instinctively moved closer to Matt. He put his arm behind her back in a gesture of support rather than intimacy. She let herself lean into him, just a little.

The ancient voodoo queen began to sway. She clapped her hands very softly to the drum's rhythm. Another drum joined in, one with a different voice that seemed to harmonize with the first.

The crone tapped her feet on the hard-packed sand. When she twirled around, Kerry saw she wore no shoes, but a circle of bells surrounded her ankles and continued down her arch, anchored by a string around her toe.

Kerry recalled seeing something similar in the tourist shops during her afternoon explorations. The string was stretchy and some of the "shoes" had plastic flowers or ribbons instead of bells for decoration.

The ceremony continued with songs and dances that were sometimes slow and gentle, sometimes wild and sensuous.

And the drums, always the drums.

Kerry found herself clapping and swaying with the crowd and Matt joined in, too, but more slowly than she did, as if he considered each action before he did it.

At one point the old queen and her retinue of young novices sprinkled exotic-smelling flower petals over the audience, an obvious blessing, and Kerry was touched by the beauty of the ceremony.

Then there were the moments of wild ecstasy when the women moved like spirits possessed by the music of tambourines and chimes and the ever-present drumbeat.

The old queen was magnificent, weaving her way among the younger women, as agile as any of them as she leaped high as the flames or swayed like a wheat stalk in the breeze. She came close to Kerry and Matt and twirled the striped cape above her head, the stirred air wafting over their faces.

A strange excitement rushed through Kerry. She was intensely aware of Matt beside her. She felt his warmth as well as that from the fire. When she gazed into the fathomless eyes of the queen, knowledge flashed between them.

Kerry and Matt would be lovers.

It was fated. Kerry knew that with an unshakable certainty, and she also knew this magic wouldn't harm her.

Sorrow sifted through her as she thought back to the previous day. Patti should have been here, leaping and swaying and whirling to the magic rhythm.

Kerry resolved to ask the old woman if they could do anything for Patti, for Queen Patrice, to assure she found peace in her death.

A large, warm hand covered hers. She glanced up at Matt and saw the question in his eyes. He must have sensed her sadness at the thought of the beautiful young woman who apparently had no one to mourn her passing.

I mourn you, Kerry said to Patti's spirit, feeling that it was close at this moment. If Patti had lived, Kerry knew they could have become lifelong friends.

"You okay?" Matt asked.

"Yes," she said. "I'll explain later." A restlessness as well as a certainty was growing inside her. She intended to use the rest of her time in New Orleans to find out about Patti and to see that she was laid to rest in a place she would have liked, not shoved into some anonymous grave in a pauper's cemetery.

Somehow Kerry would find a way to reconnect the lovely young woman she'd known so briefly with those who had loved her. Somehow she would do this, Kerry vowed.

"THIS WAY," the crone said when the ceremony was over and the fire mostly embers.

Matt moved protectively toward Kerry.

The old queen smiled slightly, then nodded her head toward the path through the trees. "I'll light the way for you." She poked a torch into the fire pit. It flamed up at once. "Come."

Matt guided Kerry in front of him on the path as they followed the woman away from the bayou. The night was eerily dark. The moon, which was full a few days ago, had disappeared behind thick white clouds during the healing ritual. The old woman with her torch was their only companion along the path. The other guests had departed quickly.

Matt hoped the cab was there as promised. Kerry had been spooked enough for one night. She seemed to be taking all this voodoo stuff rather seriously. That, plus the effect of Patti's death on her, worried him. He didn't want her gentle soul to be bruised by all this.

What was he thinking? He hardly knew Kerry, after all. Maybe both of them were affected by the tragedy more than they realized.

"Did you know Queen Patrice from the voodoo museum?" Kerry now asked the older woman.

She turned to face them. "I have been her spiritual advisor for over a year."

"Oh," Kerry said. "Then…then you must know she died last night?"

Matt observed the quick signs of shock—the blink

of the eyes, the tightening of the hand holding the torch—before the woman recovered. "I didn't. What was the cause?"

"The police aren't sure, perhaps an overdose. Do you know if she was on drugs?"

"She was not," the woman said emphatically. "It would have been a betrayal of the healing spirit." She paused. "It is her guiding spirit. She should have been here tonight."

"Did she have any family?" Kerry continued. "The police detective said she would be put in a public grave if no one claimed the body."

Matt was surprised at Kerry's persistence, then realized he shouldn't have been. She had strong feelings about family and was apparently determined to do something about Patti's lack of one.

"She must be cleansed," the woman said, the lines of her face drawn into a fierce frown. "Only fire will do that now."

"What do you mean?" Kerry asked.

"She must be cremated. Her ashes must be returned to a place of rest for her."

Kerry nodded. "Where? Where was she from?"

The voodoo queen continued along the path, muttering to herself, and didn't answer. Matt felt himself growing impatient.

Hearing steps behind them, he glanced over his shoulder. One of the younger women who'd taken part in the dancing followed them, a flashlight in her hand. She smiled and nodded.

The world felt normal once more. The old queen could sure give a person the willies.

Near the edge of the trees, the path split, and Matt spotted a familiar light by the road. Their driver had returned as promised. The old woman took the path leading back among the trees.

"This way," the younger one said, guiding them toward the taxi.

"Did you know Patti?' Kerry asked her. "She was also Queen Patrice."

"Yes. She was my friend." She was silent for a moment. "Do you know how she died?"

"Not yet—the authorities will do an autopsy," Kerry said. "There seems to be no family."

Matt studied the young voodoo queen as she paused and gazed at Kerry. She was unusually still for a moment.

"May I read your fortune?" she asked.

Kerry's shoulders stiffened. "It isn't necessary. Patti did that yesterday."

The darkly outlined eyes looked from Kerry to Matt. "Sorrow lies in your path," she said softly.

"The shining path?" Kerry questioned. "I know about that."

The young queen ignored her. "Patti sometimes spoke of a plantation where she was raised. Cordon Rouge was its name. On Bayou Rouge. The museum may know more."

With that, she turned and disappeared into the trees, the flicker of the small flashlight the only sign of her progress. Matt and Kerry were left standing in the dark.

"Well," he said, "looks like we're on our own."

"The path is fairly straight from here to the road," Kerry told him. She hurried forward.

He caught her hand and walked beside her. The trail broadened, but still Matt felt foolishly protective of the petite woman who held his hand as if she were comforted by his touch.

"What did you think?" the cabbie asked. He flicked away a cigarette and opened the door for them. "Did you find the ceremony interesting?"

"Very," Kerry said.

As they drove back to the hotel, Matt relaxed, realizing that he'd been tense for the past two hours.

"The old queen can be very haughty at times," the driver said. "I've known her to send away folks if she doesn't like them. Tourists get angry when that happens, but it isn't their call."

"Maybe they don't understand the ceremony isn't a show put on for their benefit," Kerry suggested.

"You got that right," the man said.

When she slid her hand from his, Matt resisted an urge to slip his arm around her shoulders and hold her close.

They lapsed into silence for the remainder of the trip, which seemed shorter on the return leg. At the hotel, Matt said, "I'm hungry. I've heard the chef here makes outstanding desserts. Shall we try a couple?"

Her smile almost caused his lungs to squeeze shut. "Dessert sounds wonderful. We didn't eat a lot at dinner," she reminded him.

"I hope they don't put peppers in the pies," he grumbled good-naturedly.

They laughed as they entered the restaurant. After they'd ordered decaffeinated coffee and asked for the dessert menu, Matt was pleased to see the smile linger on Kerry's expressive face as she looked around.

"The hotel is quieter tonight," she said. "I wonder if word got around about…everything."

"I suspect it has. This afternoon when I returned from the wine tasting I saw more people checking out. Some of them were probably scheduled to leave, but one couple said they'd cut their trip short because of all the weird things the night before. Their room was vandalized, too."

She nodded. "Having the generator fail in a major blackout reflects badly on the hotel. And then…then Patti."

"It was a strange first night in New Orleans," he concluded, echoing her solemn tone. "But there were a couple of good things, too."

She glanced at him in question.

"I met a lovely and helpful woman," he said, his voice going husky. "That was a plus. We saw an interesting ceremony tonight and I'm sure glad I had company for that."

Her expression brightened. "Me, too. I think I would have been frightened if I'd been alone."

The look in her eyes made him feel like a hero. He picked up the menu. "Let's check the desserts out. Maybe we should order one of everything."

"No way. We'd be on a sugar high until dawn." She quickly scanned the dessert list. "Oh my. Check out Chef Remy's specials."

Matt read over the listings on the menu. Remy Marchand, who had died in a car accident several years ago, had invented a dessert for each of his four daughters.

"Crème brûlée à la Charlotte, made with bourbon and a praline topping," he read aloud. "That's the hotel manager's name—Charlotte Marchand, the woman we met last night."

"Neapolitan pour Sylvie," Kerry took up the recitation, "three kinds of ice cream with a drizzle of white and dark chocolate on top and an almond tuile cookie on the side."

"Pavlova Renee is a frozen meringue filled with warm raspberry-peach sauce, served with Chantilly cream and fresh raspberries. Man, that sounds great. I ate pavlova every place we had dinner in Australia when my family took a vacation there. That was years ago," he added at the thoughtful glance Kerry gave him.

"Wait till you hear this one," she said with a teasing grin. "Piquante Melanie. A molten chocolate brownie on a bed of sweet cream and laced with the slightest touch of chili peppers."

They burst into spontaneous laughter. Kerry fanned her mouth with her hand as she had at the Cajun restaurant when her tongue was burning from the spicy food.

Matt caught the envious glance of a couple of men at a nearby table. Instinctively he lifted his hand to lay it over Kerry's, a gesture that would tell the men this woman was *his,* then stopped himself in time.

Back off, he warned his libido, suppressing the possessive urges he kept experiencing around her.

"Okay, that's the one for me," he told her, "Piquante Melanie. Definitely."

She sighed. "I want some of each."

When the waiter came back, Matt asked, "Would it be possible to get a sample of each of Chef Remy's specials? They all sound so delicious, we can't decide."

"Of course."

"And a glass of milk, please," Kerry requested.

The waiter nodded. "You, too, sir?"

"Why not?" Matt said, as if drinking milk at midnight was a daring feat, which caused Kerry to laugh.

When they were alone, Kerry explained that her grandparents had run a dairy farm and she'd grown up drinking milk at every meal. "It just seems to go with dessert."

He thought of the five-course dinners, a different wine served with each course, that were typical for formal occasions with his family. Otherwise meals had often been trays for him and his sister in their shared sitting room. Their parents would either be out for the evening, or ensconced in their suites, preferring to be alone rather than with their children, or even each other.

Forcing the memory from his mind, he studied Kerry. It sounded old-fashioned to say she was wholesome, but that was the term that came to mind and lingered—Kerry was "whole" in mind and spirit, loving and caring toward others, yet with an appealing independence and spunkiness he liked.

The squeezing sensation attacked his chest again. He tried to figure out why, and knew it had something to do with Kerry.

"Look at that!" she said suddenly. "It's a work of art. I'm not sure we should eat it."

The waiter grinned as he placed a huge platter in the center of the table. Each dessert sample had its own plate or crystal bowl. Flowers, fruit and fresh watercress decorated the platter.

"You must taste each one," he told them, arranging dessert plates and silverware before them, "and give me your opinion on the best."

"We will," she promised, picking up the fork.

After the server placed glasses of milk on the table and refilled their coffee cups, he left them with an admonition to "enjoy!"

"How can we help but enjoy?" she said. "Which do you want to start with?"

"Maybe the spicy one? Or should we save it for last, the pièce de résistance?"

"Let's see how hot it is," she suggested wryly.

"You first." Matt broke off a piece of the brownie with his fork, raked it through the thick layer of cream and held it out to Kerry. With a grin, he dared her to taste it.

She bravely took the bite, chewed thoughtfully, then pronounced it one of the best things she'd ever eaten.

Matt found himself staring at her lips as she licked the cream off. He had to swallow hard before he could take a bite of the treat. He could only imagine how creamy and chocolaty her lips would taste right at that moment.

They dispensed with the formality of dessert plates and ate directly from the platter. They tasted each item, argued over which was the very best, couldn't decide, then had to taste everything all over again.

Shortly after midnight, they headed for their suites, leaving half of each dessert uneaten, but not because they hadn't tried. "I am *so* full," she told him as they crossed the courtyard. "Maybe we should swim laps to work off the calories."

He looked her over. "I don't think you need to worry about that."

She gave him a startled, then pleased glance.

After opening the gate to her patio, he followed her inside, meaning only to make sure she was safe in her room before leaving her.

"Thank you for going to the ceremony," she said as she unlocked the door and pushed it open.

The night-light disclosed the turned-down bed, a frilly paper cup of mints and chocolates on the pillow.

The pleasure-pain of hot and immediate desire plunged through Matt. He wanted to lift her into his arms, kick the door shut and stay in that room—in that bed—with her for about a week, maybe two.

"I know this is too soon…" he murmured, his voice dropping to a deep, sensual level as he took her into his arms.

Her perfectly shaped mouth rounded in surprise, but she didn't pull away.

Unless she said or indicated a definite no, he knew he wouldn't stop. He had to have one taste. Her lips had tempted him almost beyond control with each bite of the luscious desserts they'd shared.

And then he couldn't think further.

Her mouth was warm. It tasted of chocolate and cream and the rich roasted flavor of expensive coffee. She was exquisite, a perfect fit in his arms. He gathered her closer, then simply lifted her off her feet so he could experience every lovely curve of her petite frame.

Hearing laughter out in the courtyard, he stepped deeper into the shadows of a potted tree, its branches arching over them like an umbrella of privacy.

She made a little keening sound, so he took the kiss deeper, invading her mouth with his tongue, searching out the sweet nectar of her. When she responded, a tad hesitant at first, then giving more…and more…he had to fight the urge to move inside to find comfort and delight in that big bed.

His leg touched something solid. A bench. He sat down on it, Kerry in his lap, a hand on his chest.

Matt wanted to rip his shirt off so she could touch his bare skin. He caressed her back, her side, then filled his palm with her perfectly shaped breast. Bliss, he thought through the red, smoky haze of increasing hunger. "Kerry," he murmured.

She stiffened and went absolutely still. "I think... perhaps...it's late," she said in a shaken tone.

He immediately released her and set her on her feet. "You're right. I should go." He paused, hoping she would contradict him, but knew she wasn't going to. "Good night, Kerry. It was a very interesting evening."

"Yes, I had a lovely time," she said, managing to sound both sincere yet stiffly polite.

As soon as she was inside her room, he closed the door, heard the lock fall into place and hurried next door.

Glancing around his own room, he noticed all was blessedly normal—no strange woman in his bed, no clothing or furniture disturbed, the light of the table lamp softly welcoming.

"And no Kerry," he muttered, surprising himself. He'd known her one day and he missed her already?

Get real.

CHAPTER FIVE

KERRY YAWNED, then took another sip of hot coffee. It was seven o'clock. She'd been awake since six. Her mind seemed fuzzy, yet filled with details of the previous evening—specifically the kiss.

When Matt kissed her, she'd nearly lost control. Odd behavior for her. But even stranger was that, after going into her room, she wished she hadn't stiffened up.

She had to laugh at herself. Most people regretted acting impulsively. *She* regretted that instant of hesitation.

Mentally shaking her head at the thought, she could almost hear the cackle of knowing laughter from the old voodoo queen. It was remembering that feeling about her and Matt becoming lovers that had made her go rigid last night. It was an enticing prospect, but the possibility it was predestined made her feel out of control.

Matt probably thought she was beyond weird.

She sighed. He was the most attractive man she'd met in ages and in more ways than just the physical.

He was kind and caring. However, she had to admit she'd had erotic dreams about him all night, so the physical was pretty compelling—

"Hello, neighbor," came a friendly voice over the fence that divided the two patios.

"Matt, hello," she said, her hand involuntarily clenching her cup. She sloshed a couple of drops of coffee on the table mat. Nothing like appearing sanguine and composed.

"Mind if I come over?" he asked.

She mopped up the drops with a napkin. "Not at all."

He left his patio and entered hers. "You're up early this morning."

"Yes. I couldn't, uh…the day seemed too beautiful to waste in sleep." She gave him a bright smile.

"I agree."

She saw him inhale deeply, then breathe out slowly. He looked solemn. She steeled herself for whatever he said. No matter what it was, she would remain calm and pleasant.

"I wanted to apologize for last night," he said, his eyes, as blue as the sky that formed a backdrop behind his head, never wavering from hers.

She nodded as she tried to think of something to say that wouldn't sound ridiculous, such as: *But I loved it!*

"Coming on to an unwilling woman isn't usually my style," he continued after the tense silence.

"No, no," she quickly assured him, "I wasn't unwilling, Matt." He had to believe her. "It was the intensity that took me by surprise."

He stared into her eyes as if determined to find the truth. "Then you forgive me?"

"There's nothing to forgive," she said firmly. "Would you care to join me? I can recommend the day's special, if you haven't had breakfast."

"Thanks, I'd like that."

He took a seat opposite her at the table. The morning air was still cool, but the sun's rays warmed her back.

The early hour and daylight didn't diminish his good looks, she noted, glancing across the table at him. He had a lean, clean-shaven face with interesting planes and a strong jaw. She liked the fact that he looked directly into her eyes when he spoke to her.

Before she could suggest he call room service, the waiter who'd served her earlier appeared with a fresh pot of coffee and a place setting on a tray.

"Will you be having breakfast, sir?" he asked, filling the cup for Matt after asking his preference for regular or decaffeinated coffee.

"Regular, please, and I'll take the special," Matt said, gesturing toward Kerry's used dishes, which the waiter loaded on the tray.

"Very good. Do you also want milk?"

Matt's blue eyes twinkled, and a smile played around the corners of his very attractive mouth. "Just orange juice."

After the waiter left, Kerry said, "The ceremony was eerie, wasn't it? The drums and the fire, the dancing and the voodoo. Perhaps it had a greater influence on us than we realized when we, I mean, last night..."

He nodded. "Perhaps," he said slowly. "But I found you hard to resist long before the ceremony."

His words filled her with the wildest surge of longing she'd ever experienced. She concentrated on her coffee cup so he wouldn't see the hunger in her eyes.

While she had normal impulses when it came to men, she didn't consider herself overly passionate. At least, she wasn't inclined to leap into bed with every handsome man she met. But where Matt was concerned, well, she kept getting ideas.

"We've shared a lot in a short time," she reminded him, as he had her. "It makes for an unexpected closeness. Or else New Orleans is working its magic on us."

"Black magic or white?" he asked wryly.

She met his gaze with a level one of her own. "I don't know." She hesitated. "I do know that I want to find out about Patti, where she was from, what will happen to her...to the remains."

"Do you want to see if the authorities will let us arrange for a cremation?"

"Could we?" she asked, giving him a hopeful look. "We also need to find out the location of the plantation that woman mentioned last night."

"So we can put her spirit to rest there," he finished.

Kerry was touched that he understood her thoughts

completely. "It's important. I don't know why. I've never believed in voodoo or anything like that, but I would like to do that for her. There was something about her that made me feel I knew her much better than I did. She was so kind to me, and I can't bear the thought that no one cares, that no one grieves for her."

Thinking of her own close-knit family, Kerry couldn't fathom having no one to mourn a death.

"Maybe we can find someone," he said. "Let's check with the museum and see what they know about her since the restaurant didn't have much information."

"Good idea."

The waiter brought Matt's breakfast. For the next hour, Kerry and Matt made plans.

KERRY STOPPED in front of the museum, reluctant to enter, as if bad news awaited her if she went inside.

"Something wrong?" Matt asked in his discerning manner.

"It was only two days ago that I first came here, Saturday afternoon at two o'clock as Patti suggested. It seems much longer."

"Because so much has happened since then," he said, holding the door for her.

They went inside. As before, burning incense sticks filled the air with spicy odors. Beneath that, the smell of mold permeated the old house, reminding her of decay and death. She hadn't particularly noticed that on Saturday.

Standing beside the table where she'd had tea with Patti, she waited for someone to appear.

Footsteps on the stairs told her someone was coming from the upper floor. A man appeared. He had a beard and long hair. Both were streaked with gray, although he didn't look over forty.

"Hello," he said with a friendly smile.

Kerry was relieved to see that he was dressed in well-faded jeans and a T-shirt, although a tiny gold ring pierced the edge of one eyebrow.

"Good morning," Kerry and Matt answered together.

Matt motioned for her to continue. "We're here about Patti—Queen Patrice," she added.

The man looked thoughtful and sad. "I talked to the police yesterday. The detective told me what happened. Are you friends of hers?"

"We met her recently," Matt said. "We wanted to find out if you know where she's from and if she has any family."

The man shook his head. "We told the cops all we knew, which wasn't much. My wife and I will miss her. She was a very reliable employee. The tourists liked her, too."

"She took my picture with Jolie," Kerry told him, "so I could impress my nephew."

The owner smiled. "Yes, she was great with the pythons." He studied them a second. "She didn't have any family that I know of."

"Oh," Kerry said despondently.

"You know, you might find out more about Patti at the warehouse where she was working on a Mardi Gras float. She said a friend of hers was in charge of getting part of the float done and that his father was the krewe king."

Kerry tried to relate this information to the few facts she recalled about Mardi Gras floats. The "krewe" was the sponsoring group for the float. There was always a king, usually an older, prominent citizen, and a queen or princess, often a young beautiful woman.

That sounded sexist to her, but it wasn't her concern at the moment. The detective had mentioned a boyfriend. That was the best lead they had so far. "Do you know where the warehouse is located?"

"Yes. Here, I'll show you on a map." He took a pamphlet from the table and opened it.

Kerry and Matt looked over his shoulder while he drew an X to indicate the museum and another to show them where the warehouse was located near the river but past the French Quarter. He handed them the map, which was the usual one given to visitors by shops and hotels.

"Do you know the friend's name?" Matt asked.

"Sorry, I don't. Patti was friendly with everyone, but she was reserved when it came to her personal data. However, she did tell us amusing stories about working on the float and the frustration of dealing with hundreds of volunteers."

"Thank you so much for your time," Kerry said, knowing they'd gotten all the info the man had.

Matt expressed his appreciation, too, and shook hands with the man. Outside, he and Kerry stopped under a shade tree and checked the map.

"This way," he said, pointing down the street. "It's several blocks. Do you want to walk or grab a taxi?"

"Would you mind walking? If I continue with the decadent desserts, I'm going to need the exercise."

"Okay. Let's go down to the river and stroll along it. We may as well enjoy the scenery."

When he held out his arm, she found it very natural to rest her hand in the bend of his elbow as they headed for the riverfront.

KERRY AND MATT found the street that led to the Warehouse District. The street name was Tchoupitoulas, but neither Matt nor Kerry knew how to pronounce it.

"After checking out the warehouse," Matt said, "we should go for a ride on a steamer, maybe have lunch aboard."

"Sounds fun. I want to tour some of the plantations, too."

"Okay, we've got a plan."

He gave her an easy smile that made her heart feel lighter and her blood warmer. Although they had to avoid areas of construction, which was still going on as a result of hurricane damage, they found an interesting mix of galleries and shops in the area.

When at last they reached the address marked on the map by the museum owner, they discovered a huge warehouse. Its doors stood wide open, and inside, volunteers swarmed over the framework of an impressive flower-bedecked float.

"I think it's a garden," Kerry said.

"It is," a young man told them, hurrying over with a clipboard in one hand and a pencil in the other. He looked to be in his early twenties, tall and attractive with black hair and light blue-gray eyes. He didn't even glance at them. "Whose team are you on?"

"None," Matt answered. "Uh, I'm Matt Anderson. We met yesterday at your home."

"Matt, of course." The younger man switched the pencil to his other hand and shook hands with Matt, apologizing at once for not recognizing him.

"Kerry, this is Jason Pichante. His father hosted the wine-tasting I attended yesterday afternoon. Jason, Kerry Johnston. Like me, Kerry's a guest in your fair city."

"Welcome to the Big Easy," Jason said.

Kerry thought his manner somewhat preoccupied and distant even as he smiled graciously.

"Sorry, Matt, Kerry," Jason continued, "but only workers are allowed in. You're not allowed in. However, you may watch from the door as long as you don't go inside. Or you can help on the cottage garden," he suggested.

When Matt glanced at Kerry, she nodded. This was

a chance she didn't want to miss. Maybe they could find Patti's friend and he could tell them how to locate her family or at least verify that she had been alone in the world.

"Working on the float sounds like fun," Matt said. He turned to Kerry. "This will be something to brag about to our friends and families when we watch the Mardi Gras parade on television."

"We'll probably be snowed in and wish we were back here where the weather is beautiful," Kerry added ruefully.

"Let me get your names and addresses," Jason told them. "You'll have to sign releases in case of an accident."

After he got all the personal information required by insurance companies, he had them sign the city's release forms and then introduced them to his assistant, a friendly young blonde named Ashley James.

"Welcome to the crew," she said enthusiastically.

"Is that crew with a *c* or krewe with a *k?*" Kerry asked.

Ashley grinned. "With a *c*. We're just worker bees here. Jason is a member of the krewe putting the float together. His dad is the king, in fact."

"What shall we do?" Matt asked before Kerry could say anything about Patti's boyfriend. He gave her a warning squeeze on the arm to be patient.

Kerry listened carefully to the instructions. She and Matt were assigned the task of stringing support wires between rebar poles for the "flowers" that would bloom there. Every flower on the float, they learned, would be made from actual plant material.

After working for two hours with six other people, a break was called. Sodas and iced tea were served along with Mardi Gras cakes and cookies.

"Chew carefully," Ashley said when Kerry chose one of the cakes. "Those are king cakes and have tokens in them."

"As a dental hygienist, that possibility worries me," Kerry told her. She and Matt found a place to sit with their backs against the warehouse wall.

"I'll try not to break a tooth on a trinket," he promised with a grin.

Kerry was glad she was sitting. His smile was enough to make her knees go weak, especially after they'd been working so closely all morning. Their shoulders, arms and hands had touched constantly as she held the wires in place while he twisted them around the supports with pliers.

His scent had mingled with hers, giving her heady ideas about heated caresses in a cool, dim room.

"Matt," she said, directing her thoughts to the reason they were here, "do you think Jason Pichante could be the friend mentioned by the museum owner? If his father is the krewe king, then he must be, don't you think?"

"I'm not sure. Jason is from an old New Orleans family. He probably wouldn't be involved with a waitress and voodoo queen—"

He broke off abruptly.

"What?" she demanded.

Matt reminded Kerry about the tension he'd witnessed between father and son at the wine tasting. "After Jason slammed out of the room, his father said his son thought he was in love, but the person was unsuitable."

"Like Patti," Kerry concluded, angry on her behalf. "Do you think Jason even knows she died? It must have been in the papers by now. The guy at the museum didn't mention anyone asking about her, other than the police."

"We could be wrong about the friend's identity," Matt reminded her. "We'll have to ask someone. Ashley would probably know."

Kerry nodded. She took a bite of the cake, which was a cinnamon pastry with gold, green and purple icing. "Oh-oh," she muttered. She carefully extracted a tiny object that had been in the cake. "It's like a little doll—a baby," she said.

Ashley came over and sat on the floor in front of them with a glass of iced tea and a cookie. "That's very good luck, you know. It represents the Christ Child. The Mardi Gras colors and trinkets represent the gifts of the Three Wise Men to the Baby Jesus."

"Twelfth Night is the Epiphany, the night they found the stable and presented their gifts," Matt added. "I read that in the book from the museum."

Kerry thought this was a good lead-in and gave

Matt a grateful glance. "Did you know the docent there?" she asked Ashley. "Queen Patrice?"

"Patti? Of course." Ashley looked puzzled. "She works on the float, too, but she didn't come in this morning."

"Then you don't know that she seems to have overdosed on something Saturday night?" Kerry asked.

"Overdosed," Ashley repeated. "Is she okay?"

"No. She died." Kerry noted the shock in the young woman's eyes.

"She was supposed to have worked yesterday afternoon, too," Ashley murmured. "Jason was very upset when I asked about her. Oh, my God, does he know?"

Kerry had a question of her own. "Was he Patti's boyfriend?"

Ashley stared at her without answering.

"The owner at the museum said she had a friend whose father was the krewe king," Kerry continued, "and that Patti worked on the float. That's why we came—"

"You can't ask questions," Ashley said suddenly.

"Why?" Matt asked, his tone hard.

Ashley glanced around as if expecting the secret police to pounce on them. "Jason is from a very old, very powerful family in New Orleans. They will protect their own if you try to implicate him in…in anything."

"Such as the death of a young woman he was seeing?" Matt suggested. "An inappropriate young woman?"

Tears filled Ashley's eyes. "Patti was a friend. She was from a family as old and prestigious as the Pichantes, only they lost most of their money long ago. When Patti was eight, her father lost everything they had left."

"Like what?" Matt asked.

"A plantation—terribly run-down, from what Patti said. Her father committed suicide after that. Her mother had died in an auto accident the year before."

"Did Patti go to an orphanage or into foster care?" Kerry inquired.

Ashley shook her head. "Her aunt had married money. She and her husband took Patti in. But it was a miserable life, I think," Ashley confided in a very low voice. "They didn't want her and made sure she knew it was only by their great kindness that she had a home."

"How did she meet Jason?"

"University. Her relatives had sent her to Newcombe College. It's part of Tulane. That's where all the people of their social status go, so Patti had to go there, too."

"Did she get a degree?"

"Yes, in fine arts." Ashley grimaced. "Shh, here comes Jason."

"I want to talk to him," Kerry stated.

"Be careful." Ashley rose and headed toward the refreshment table for a refill of iced tea.

Jason joined Matt and Kerry. "Are you enjoying the work on the float?" he asked.

"It's different," Matt said in an affable tone. His smile faded. "There's something we need to know."

Jason cast him a wary glance.

"We're interested in Patti Ruoui. According to the owner at the museum where she worked, Patti had a friend whose father was the krewe king on a float she worked on. The police think she also had a boyfriend. That would be you, wouldn't it?"

The younger man paled, then twin peaks of color bloomed across his cheeks. "Patti was a friend," he admitted guardedly. "We saw each other at times. She was a regular with the work crew on the float."

"So there was nothing serious between the two of you?" Matt persisted.

"No. Nothing." He rose. "It's time to get back to work. If you'll excuse me."

"Were you with her Saturday night?" Matt inquired.

"Why do you ask?" His eyes seemed to turn black as he stared at Matt, almost daring him to say more.

"Apparently she took an overdose that night and was left for dead in a hotel room." Matt paused. "Mine."

"Mon Dieu," Jason muttered. "She isn't...dead?"

Kerry caught the hesitation on the last word. Jason hadn't answered Matt's question, she noted, her suspicions aroused. If he had been with Patti Saturday, had he left her, thinking she had merely passed out?

"Yes," Matt stated flatly, "she died. The medical examiner is doing an autopsy today, I understand."

"I see. I know someone in his office. I'll call and find out if they know how she…what caused the death."

He left them without a backward glance as he went to Ashley and gave her some orders about her crew.

She nodded several times. After Jason left her, she tossed a warning glance their way, then went back to work with the other volunteers.

"Let's go," Matt said. "I think we've found out all we're going to here."

"I agree."

With a wave to Ashley, they headed out the door and into the sunshine. "It's after eleven," Matt said. "Let's see about that ride on a steamboat."

"Sounds great."

They caught a bus back to the river park and found a place to buy tickets on one of the stately river steamers. When Kerry offered to pay for her share for the ride and plantation tour, Matt eyed the bills she held, then her, but he didn't insist on playing the cosmopolitan spender from the big city, which she would have found insulting.

Another point in his favor.

The list of his virtues was growing quite long. He was more than charming; he was thoughtful in ways she hadn't noticed in the male population back in her hometown.

However, she seemed to notice a lot more about this man than she did any other. They also had an intuitive understanding of each other that was surprising and wonderful and maybe a little frightening.

Was she under some kind of spell? She silently laughed at herself as her imagination went wild.

Follow the shining path...

She inhaled slowly, carefully as her pulse went into overdrive. Was Matt her co-traveler on this great adventure, her guide to a magical interlude of romance and excitement on the strangest vacation of her life?

Mentally crossing her fingers, she hoped so. She truly hoped so.

A FEW MINUTES AFTER noon, Kerry and Matt were on a steamboat huffing its way upriver. Another boat passed them, its calliope blasting loud enough to "wake the dead," Kerry said, leaning over to shout in Matt's ear in order to be heard.

"Or perhaps the undead," he shouted back.

His lips were so close to her cheek it would have taken very little effort for him to steal a kiss, but he refrained. She wished he hadn't, or that she had enough nerve to steal one herself.

The thought filled her head with so many other possibilities as he lingered near her for another second. She sighed when he settled back in his seat.

Their food arrived. She tried to figure out how to eat the huge sandwich, which was the local version of a po' boy.

"Muffletta sandwich?" Kerry said, gazing at the

plate in awe. "This is more than four people can handle."

"Speak for yourself," Matt teased. "I'm starved after all that work on the float. I thought we were only going to spend a half hour there." He lowered his eyebrows at her.

"Well," she said loftily, "we had to gain Ashley's trust so she would talk to us." She picked up the knife and fork, approaching the giant sandwich by cutting it into bites.

"Jason was lying," Matt said. "He and Patti were much more than friends."

"I agree. Did you see how pale he went, then those red spots appeared on his cheeks as he tried to be casual about her?"

Matt nodded.

"I don't see how he could learn of her death and just walk away like that, as if it meant nothing to him."

"Perhaps it didn't," Matt said, softly now that the other boat had passed them and the music was a pleasant melody wafting on the breeze.

Kerry swallowed hard, and her eyes burned as she blinked rapidly. "He couldn't be that callous." She gazed at Matt. "Could he?"

Matt lifted one hand and stroked her cheek with the back of his fingers. "I don't know, honey. I just don't know."

CHAPTER SIX

KERRY WOKE from a short afternoon nap in a lethargic haze. For a moment, she was disoriented.

"Oh," she murmured, rising and stretching muscles that felt as if she'd run a marathon. She'd walked a lot since arriving in New Orleans and working on the float, holding those wires over her head, had strained the muscles in her arms, legs and neck.

After a tour of one of the famous plantations along the Mississippi, she and Matt had returned to the city via the steamboat. She'd opted for a nap while Matt went off on pursuits of his own without saying what they were.

She'd started to ask what he was going to do, but fortunately had stopped herself in time. In her family, everyone knew everyone else's business. They consulted and advised each other as a matter of course. Even though she felt she'd known Matt forever, he probably wouldn't appreciate the loving closeness that allowed such liberties.

She wondered if Matt had similar feelings about her. He had called her "honey" while stroking her cheek. But that might have been because he'd sensed her distress and was sympathetic.

Maybe she was imagining things, but she felt she'd bonded with both Matt and Patti for reasons she couldn't figure out. It was odd, this web of circumstances that had drawn them into the same circle.

The charms on her bracelet tinkled loudly as she rose. As she looked at the three crossed bones, a sudden chill spread over her. Three intertwined lives, one of them already ended in tragedy. What would happen to her and Matt?

Tears stung her eyes as she contemplated the possibility of something terrible happening to Matt. Pressing the heels of her hands against her eyelids, she shook her head as if defying fate and managed a soft laugh.

When had she become so morbid?

After slipping on a light sweater, she went out on her patio and peered across the courtyard. A couple of families were in the swimming pool. A bit cool for that, in her opinion. Others sat at the outdoor tables and chairs and chatted.

She went to the courtyard bar, ordered a raspberry iced tea and returned to her room. The gate was open to the next-door patio suite, the one where Matt had first stayed. She looked in.

"Detective Rothberg," she said upon recognizing him.

He turned from taking the yellow police tape off the

door. "Hello," he said. "I recognize your face, but the name escapes me at the moment."

"Kerry Johnston. I'm next door." She pointed toward the middle suite.

"Of course. From Minnesota."

"Yes. Uh, have you learned anything about Patti? Has the autopsy been done yet?"

He nodded. "That's why I'm taking down the tape. We're through with the investigation."

Kerry was shocked. "But why?"

"There was no crime. Miss Ruoui wasn't murdered, which is what I first thought."

"So it was an overdose," Kerry murmured. Patti's voodoo friends had been wrong about her drug use.

"You might say so." The detective rolled the tape into a ball and stuck it in his jacket pocket. "But not from drugs. She had a severe allergic reaction to an ingredient in a love potion she drank."

"A love potion," Kerry repeated and thought of handsome, angry, moody Jason Pichante.

"Yes. My partner and I pieced the evening together. The bartender and a couple of the servers remembered seeing Miss Ruoui and her escort since they were dressed in black with white faces. It's a common representation of Death during Mardi Gras."

"I see."

"They joined the crowd in the courtyard shortly before the electricity went off."

"Yes, I remember couples from the hotel's Twelfth

Night party coming out to the courtyard, plus others from the street."

He smiled grimly. "Yeah, that's the Big Easy. There're no boundaries. Everybody crashes. Anyway, an old woman circulated through the crowd selling voodoo spells. Apparently Miss Ruoui's date bought two of the popular love potions. One of the servers recalled them teasing each other, then they both drank the potions."

"He didn't die," Kerry said, almost resentful of that fact.

"He wasn't allergic to the roots and herbs used in the potion. According to the medical examiner it was a common concoction, but the victim went into anaphylactic shock almost immediately. When she felt ill, she probably went searching for the ladies room. Instead she stumbled into this patio. When she saw the door was open, she went inside to lie down until she felt better."

"Wouldn't she have been afraid the occupant might return at any moment?" Kerry asked.

"People usually party until the wee hours," he said with a shake of his head. "And I doubt she was thinking clearly by then. She was certainly in no shape to consider the consequences."

"Did she die quickly? And painlessly?"

"Well, she would have known something was seriously wrong, but yes, she went quickly. The air passages close up so the person passes out pretty fast."

"That's why the CPR didn't work," Kerry said. "I tried but it didn't do any good."

Kerry knew about allergic reactions. One of her dental patients had had a severe reaction to a numbing compound the dentist had given her before drilling in a molar. Fortunately the paramedics had been able to save her.

The detective checked the room before closing the door. "The investigation is closed as of now," he told her with an air of finality.

"What about Patti's date? Did you talk to him?"

Detective Rothberg hesitated before saying, "My partner handled that end of things. Since we know she voluntarily took the potion, there'll be no further query into the case."

Kerry noted he didn't answer her directly or mention a name. Was he covering for the powerful Pichante family? "Since she appears to have no next of kin, is a friend allowed to claim the remains?"

"You can check with the medical examiner's office on that." He pulled out a card and wrote on the back. "Here's the number. The woman who answers is the department executive assistant. She probably knows more about the rules and regulations than anyone. Ask her."

"Thank you." Kerry tucked the card in her pocket.

"Better wait until the morning. She'll be gone by now. The office opens at eight."

"Right."

After he left, two maids entered the suite and started a thorough cleaning. Kerry hurried to her room. She could hardly wait until Matt returned so she could share this news. She left a message on his voice mail to call her.

MATT LISTENED attentively as Kerry told him about the detective releasing his former quarters. Her hazel eyes flickered with the fire of indignation.

"I know this is sadistic of me, but I hope Jason—assuming he's the person who abandoned Patti, and I'm sure he is—was grilled by the cops the way they do in crime dramas on television. The detective never did say Jason was questioned, though, only that his partner had handled that part of the investigation.

"According to witnesses, Patti drank the potion voluntarily," Kerry continued. "So did her date. Since neither appeared to have been forced, that ended the matter as far as the police were concerned. It really was an accident. I'm glad to know that."

"Yes. It must have been terrible for Patti, though."

She told Matt of the dental patient who'd gone into anaphylactic shock so severe the emergency medical team had had to open the woman's trachea right there in the dentist's office before taking her to the hospital.

"I remember how frightened she was when she couldn't breathe," Kerry said. "She clawed at her throat…"

Matt laid a hand over Kerry's, the need to comfort her too great to ignore.

"Sorry," she said. "I'm getting all emotional. Anyway, I hope Jason was scared. He deserves to feel as frightened as Patti must have been when she became ill." She paused as if shocked at her words. "I didn't realize I was so vindictive," she said in a low voice.

"Not vindictive," Matt corrected, reluctantly removing his hand from hers. "You want justice."

It was strange how much he wanted to touch Kerry. Part of it was sensual, yes, but there was more to it than that. He felt a bond with her, and a need to comfort her. But most of all he felt pure pleasure at connecting with her.

All these feelings were foreign to him. Usually he kept himself aloof from other people's emotions. It was just that she was so real, so warm.

He watched as she fingered the cool petal of a flower, her mood introspective. Something drew him to this lovely woman in ways he couldn't fully explain. Was it her concern for others? Her down-to-earth approach to life? Her obvious love for her family and the closeness they seemed to share? These were aspects of her life that had been absent from his for a long, long time.

Pushing the useless musing aside, he sternly reminded himself that they'd barely met. First impressions were often wrong, as he'd learned from his former fiancée. Things, or people, that seemed too good to be true often were.

He focused on the situation at hand.

"It's sad that no one seems interested in what became of Patti," Kerry said, her eyes so beautiful, so filled with pity, he wanted to take her in his arms.

"We're interested," he assured her.

"I have a number to call in the morning to find out about the body—what will happen to it," she added when he raised his eyebrows in question.

"I've been doing some investigating on my own," he told her. "I went to Tulane University and checked their records for the past few years."

"I didn't think of that. What did you find out?"

"That she graduated four years ago and would have been twenty-six in June. That she was smart and had a full academic scholarship. That she worked in the registrar's office to earn her spending money. If she had help with finances, it apparently wasn't much."

"Was all that in her records?"

"No, but the woman who worked there remembered Patti and was shocked at her death. She joined me for a break and we had a lengthy chat over coffee."

Kerry surprised him by leaning over and giving him a hug. "I'm so glad *someone* remembered Patti."

Her lips were just too close and too tempting. Matt took advantage of the moment and claimed the prize.

Her mouth was soft beneath his. Just as he remembered. Her lips trembled a tiny bit. Just as he remembered. She opened to him when he stroked his tongue over the sweet line of her mouth. Just as he remembered.

Although it was difficult not to become lost in passion, part of him was aware that they weren't in the most private place in the world. There was a courtyard nearby where other guests chatted, read or swam in the pool. He pulled back from her.

Their eyes met, and he was reminded of the green waters of the Caribbean, rocky pools tucked in among the sandy beaches. He looked away as memories flowed into his mind like waves.

His family had been to the Virgin Islands many times for summer vacations. Left to their own devices, he and his sister had explored to their heart's content. It had been fun...

For the first time in years, he realized how much he missed their companionship. The two of them had been close as children and as adults, although she was four years older. Until she'd graduated from college and gone to Africa, she'd always been there for him.

He covertly studied Kerry. Was she the one to fill the empty places in his life, to be the companion he hadn't fully realized he missed until he met her?

Hmm, maybe Romeo and Juliet had fallen in love at first sight, but he knew both he and Kerry were more cautious.

However, the attraction between them was growing stronger with every hour of the day as they worked to solve the mystery of Patti's past, this unknown woman who just might have changed their lives forever...

Clearing his throat, he said, "I've been invited to din-

ner at a country club just outside the city tonight.
There'll be a wine tasting afterward. I was told to bring
a guest if I wanted. I'd like to take you, if you're interested?"

She blinked as if caught off-guard by the question.
"I'm not sure I should," she said. "This is work for you.
I don't want to get in the way."

He chuckled. "You won't. I'll take notes and act as
if you aren't even in the room."

That made her smile. "I've been to some wineries
in California so I'm familiar with the protocol of a
wine tasting," she assured him.

A smile teased the corners of her mouth, so he was
prepared as she continued on a droll note.

"I do have one question. Do I swish the wine clock-
wise or counterclockwise before I spit it on the carpet?"

"I believe I read a story about that when I took
American literature in college," he informed her.

"Yeah, so did I, but it's fun putting you on."

"Do you think I'm a stuffed shirt?" he demanded.

She shook her head, her spiky hair gleaming in the
dappled late-afternoon sun, making him want to touch
it, to muss it up and smooth it out…

"However, I do want to remind you that a small-
town dental hygienist from the Midwest may be intimidated by those who live on a, shall we say, loftier
plane."

"Ha," he said to that.

"Okay, I won't be," she admitted, "but if you see me

trapped by some society matron telling me of all the Mardi Gras balls on her social calendar this season, I expect an immediate rescue."

"It's a promise." He held out his hand.

When she put her hand in his, he did what seemed natural. He lifted it to his lips and kissed each slender knuckle.

MATT HAD a startling revelation when he picked up Kerry for their gala evening—he was going to have a much harder time keeping his hands to himself than he'd thought.

She was enchanting in a long black skirt, a camisole top in gold with bugle beads that shimmered with each breath she took, and an elegant silk scarf, black interwoven with gold, purple and green, draped casually around her neck.

Her eyes seemed as large as the lanterns glowing on a nearby patio and were skillfully outlined in black with green-and-gold shadows highlighting them. A man could drown in those eyes and never regret it…

"Is this okay?" she asked a trifle anxiously. "I bought the scarf the first day I arrived…"

He realized he'd been staring too long. "Perfect," he assured her, his voice dropping an octave.

Other parts of his body also reacted. He couldn't help that, but in every other way, he would exert control, he told his libido sternly.

The town car he'd ordered was waiting in front of

the hotel. He helped Kerry inside, making sure her skirt was tucked in before the driver closed the door. He held her hand as if they were a couple on a prom date. The trip was much too short.

At the country club, he noted Kerry taking in her lush surroundings. He tried to see the place through her eyes, but it only reminded him of his youth. The lobby and dining room featured cream-colored marble columns and green-and-mauve carpets on granite floor tiles. Both rooms were decorated in different colors but in the same tastefully understated style as the country club his family belonged to.

A man in a dark evening suit approached them, hand outstretched. He and Matt greeted each other, then Matt introduced Kerry. "Terrence Wilson is the president of the country club," he explained. "He arranged the review of their cellar."

"How thoughtful," Kerry said. "I'm looking forward to the evening."

"Glad you could join us," the man replied in the friendly manner Matt had found throughout the city. He led the way to a table with a great view of the river.

The moon cast a quicksilver path over the water's black, ever shifting surface. Matt inhaled slowly, deeply. The river, the moonlight and the woman beside him were so lovely, it made his insides tighten up in a way he'd never experienced before.

As he seated Kerry, he noted there were three other people at the table, a man and two women.

Terrence introduced his wife, Jessica, a woman in her fifties whose smile was friendly. The other woman was their daughter, a blonde with the glowing tan of a very expensive salon. Her name was Chandra. She had blue, predatory eyes.

Matt could have given an instant profile of the woman. Around thirty. Divorced. Bored. She looked him over as if he were a morsel she might be tempted to sample.

He gave an invisible shudder. No, thanks, he could have told her. He'd met her type in a hundred other cities.

The other man was Terrence's nephew, the male version of Chandra, who also had blue, restless eyes. Matt's smile became genuine as Kerry shook hands and spoke to each person, her manner easy and charming. She was neither intimidated nor impressed.

Over cocktails, he and Kerry answered questions about their activities in the city. With only a bit of exaggeration for effect, he described the healing ceremony and how spooky it was, right next door to the cemetery.

The blonde touched his arm. "It's nice that you're having an adventure," she said, her interest so obvious Matt found himself irritated by it.

He laid a hand over Kerry's, which rested on the table. "I'm glad Kerry was with me at the ritual. She had her picture taken with a python at one of the voodoo museums, so I knew she had lots of the good *Ju-Ju.*"

"Oh, lots," Kerry said, smiling ruefully as the others laughed.

The older woman studied Kerry as if she took the discussion seriously. "That's very good *Ju-Ju* indeed. The snake represents the Spirit of Wisdom. The python must have recognized a kindred spirit in you."

"I like that idea," Kerry said. She held up her wrist with the bracelet. "I'll have to get a snake charm before I leave New Orleans."

The soft light cast a glow over Kerry's face. Matt decided she was the most beautiful woman in the room. He wished they were alone in a quiet private place to see where this attraction might lead.

He also made a note to purchase the charm for her.

The dinner, steak and the region's famous crayfish, was a success. They sampled a variety of wines with each course, and Matt made notes on each. After the entree, he and Kerry accompanied their host on a tour of the cellars, located in a salt cave under the main building.

"The salt is many feet thick, formed in the marsh over thousands of years," Terrence explained. "It's been reinforced with concrete pillars, so it's safe."

He opened three bottles for further sampling. The wines were French and had been laid down in a vintage season several years ago. "We have one case of each left. I want your opinion. Are they still drinkable?"

The first one had gone to vinegar. Matt and Terrence laughed as Kerry grimaced upon tasting it.

"I think we can rule this one out," Terrence said.

The other two were fine. Matt noted that Kerry took only the tiniest sip of each one. He poured the remainder of each wine into the waste receptacle, and she did the same. After that, they returned to the dining room, where bananas Foster were prepared at the table.

Kerry, her eyes shining, was served first and invited to give her opinion of the rich dessert. She tried a bite and pronounced it "perfect."

When the waiter brought more wine, Kerry laid her fingers over her glass to indicate she'd had enough.

Matt remembered the story of her uncle, who'd shown what could come from excessive drinking. She was practicing what her family had preached, he realized.

In two days, he'd shared more with Kerry than with women he'd known for a much longer time. She'd told him about the cousin who'd committed suicide, and he'd talked about the death of his sister. It didn't even seem odd.

Would this closeness disappear when they returned to their respective homes?

While he contemplated this, a small orchestra began playing. Many couples rose and headed for the dance floor.

"Would you excuse us?" Matt said to the others, taking Kerry's hand. Whether it was wise or not, he had to have her in his arms. Now.

He led her to the dance floor and she gazed up at

him, a smile on her lips and in her eyes, as they began to move to the slow rhythm of a love song.

"You're incredibly beautiful," he said.

Her smile widened. "Thank you, kind sir."

Her voice held laughter…and secrets…and promises that would never be broken.

Something fierce grabbed his heart and wouldn't let go. He wanted to hold her close, but the difference in their heights precluded it. If they had been alone, he would simply have lifted her off her feet.

Realizing she was a very good dancer, he changed up their steps, spinning her around, bringing her to his side so they faced the same direction, then spinning her out again. She followed effortlessly, and he increased the intricacy of their movements.

"You like to dance," she said in delight. "And you're good. Every woman here will be hoping you'll ask them next."

He shook his head. "There's only one woman I want."

She caught her lower lip between her teeth for a second as if suppressing a gasp, then she gave him a mock frown.

"You shouldn't say things like that," she murmured, then added, "when we're in a crowd."

When she looked up at him and laughed, he saw the impish gleam in those verdant depths. The giant fist squeezed his heart again.

At the end of the dance, he pushed a pager in his

pocket that would alert their driver, checked his notes with Terrence, told the others he'd been very pleased to have met them and escorted Kerry out of the building. The town car stopped just as they reached the portico.

"How did he know we were ready?" she asked.

Matt grinned. "Magic."

On the twenty-minute drive to the hotel, Kerry snuggled into Matt's side, her head against his arm. She yawned.

"I had a wonderful time, Matt," she murmured sleepily.

"Are you falling asleep on me?" he asked. "I should have monitored your wine intake more closely."

"Three glasses," she said. "And one cocktail. I kept count. One glass an hour maximum." She yawned again.

"Good girl."

"You're bigger than I am, so your body can process more in a shorter time. But not too much more," she lectured.

"Right," he said, laughter in his voice.

He laid his cheek on her head and looped his arm around her shoulders. Beneath the cool silk of the scarf, he could feel the warmth of her skin. Heat spread in waves from every point where they touched. He allowed himself to enjoy the sensations.

At the hotel, he kept his arm around her as they made their way through the lobby and across the softly lit courtyard. It was after midnight, but there was a couple near the pool, and a few others scattered in the shadows under the potted palms, their conversations muted.

Inside Kerry's patio, Matt held her while she felt around in her evening purse for the key. He took it from her and opened the door, then realized he wasn't ready to let her go, not just yet.

"Kerry," he said.

She looked up at him. The moonlight shone in her eyes while a slight smile curved her mouth into enticing lines. "Yes," she whispered, as if answering a question.

The temptation was too great. He took her into his arms and claimed the treasure of her mouth, devouring all the sweetness within until he was lost to reason.

"Oh, Matt," she said when he kissed along her cheek to her ear. "I've thought of this…."

"So have I."

"Let's go inside," she said with practical good sense.

He stepped over the threshold and gave the door a push with his foot. Soft music played. The lamp was on beside the bed. The covers were turned down, ready to welcome the weary traveler to rest.

But he wasn't weary and it wasn't rest he wanted. Neither did she.

"That feels so good," she said as he stroked along her back, his hands careful on the beaded top. The scarf had slipped down so that it draped to her waist, held in place by the crook of her elbows.

He tossed it on a chair. Placing an arm behind her knees, he lifted her and sat down on the bed, holding her in his lap. She pushed his suit jacket off his shoulders and down his arms. He tossed it toward the chair, too. His tie followed.

Then he returned to her lips, consumed by the lush taste he found there.

"Mmm, mmm, mmm," she said, planting kisses all over his face, then his neck. She opened buttons and licked along his skin, setting fires wherever she touched. Her hands skimmed his flesh when she pushed his shirt aside.

He found the zipper to her top and disposed of it. Her breasts gleamed in the lamplight like the finest marble, but warm...so warm...

By mutual unspoken consent, they lay back on the broad bed, the need urgent and hot between them. She moved against him, her nipples barely brushing his chest.

Easing down, he kissed each delicate peak and laved them with his tongue, smiling as they contracted more.

"Make love to me," she said in a dreamy tone, her eyes alight with need.

And the wine she'd consumed? some wary, and perhaps more honorable, part of him wondered.

With a sigh, he knew he couldn't risk that possibility. Somehow this was too important. "Not tonight," he said, lifting himself up on his elbow so he could gaze into her face.

She looked so disappointed, he almost forgot his reservation. "Another time?" she asked in the sweet, earnest manner that he found so endearing.

He laughed softly. "You better believe it, but not when you've had three glasses of wine and a cocktail. I want to make sure you remember every detail."

"I will," she vowed.

He kissed her forehead, her nose, her mouth. "So will I, honey, and that's a fact."

Then he got himself out of there, the door safely closed and locked behind him, before he could change his mind.

CHAPTER SEVEN

KERRY PUT ON her dark glasses and a lacy-brimmed hat before joining Matt for breakfast on his patio.

He opened the gate for her, gazed into her face, then burst into laughter. "Do you need a dose of the hair of the dog that bit you?"

"No! No more wine for me," she declared, taking the seat he held out for her, one that was deeper in the shade, she noted. The morning light exacerbated the headache pinging behind her eyes. "Not ever."

He chuckled again, a sound so alluring, she had a hard time keeping her hands off him.

"Your problem is most likely dehydration. I should have told you to drink a full glass of water and take a multiple vitamin last night before you went to bed."

She nodded. "This seems to be a habit with us," she began warily, "but I think I owe you an apology this morning for, uh, my actions last night."

"Not at all. To coin a phrase, 'A pleasant time was had by all.' Especially by me," he added in a sensuous voice that reached right down and caressed a place inside her heart. He poured her a cup of coffee.

"I had a lovely evening, Matt," she told him in the most sincere manner she could muster at this early hour.

Which was actually ten o'clock.

"I took the liberty of ordering some breakfast rolls and muffins when I heard your shower come on. Do you mind?"

"No. That was thoughtful of you." She took a tiny sip of coffee, found it didn't make her queasy and took another. "You were right last night. I was more…"

She tried to think of a word that didn't make her sound like a lush.

"Happy," he supplied.

"I was much happier than I realized," she admitted ruefully. Nothing like making a fool of oneself in front of a man who was probably used to the most sophisticated women in the world. She mentally groaned.

The waiter knocked on the post next to the gate, then entered, a smile on his face. "The hair of the dog," he said, placing a tall glass of tomato juice in front of Kerry. "The chef said this would fix you right up."

"Does everyone know how *happy* I was last night?" she demanded after the waiter placed two baskets of rolls on the table, then departed.

"I was the only one with that privilege," Matt told her with an intimate glance as he poured more coffee. "However, I asked the waiter what might be soothing when a person consumed a tad more wine than usual."

"Ah, all becomes clear," she said, adopting his playful tone. Actually she did feel better.

Kerry found the tomato juice, laced with lemon and a drop of Louisiana hot sauce, really was just the thing to revitalize her appetite. She drank half of it before replacing the glass on the table and selecting a warm croissant from one of the baskets.

"Charlotte Marchand stopped by this morning," he continued. "We had a chat about Patti and the vandalism on Saturday. Apparently it was very minor—nothing valuable was stolen. She seemed to have a lot on her mind, but things have quieted down since the blackout, she said. I'm sure she was relieved Patti's death was accidental and the investigation over."

That reminded Kerry of her mission. "The detective gave me a number to call at the medical examiner's office. He said the secretary could tell me what would happen to Patti. I meant to call at eight on the dot, before the office got too busy."

"Call now," he urged.

She fished the business card and her cell phone out of her purse. The number answered on the first ring.

"Office of the Medical Examiner," a crisp feminine voice said.

Kerry explained who she was and how she got the number. "I'm a friend of Patti Ruoui. She was brought in Saturday night—"

"I have her paperwork on my desk," the woman

said, sounding efficient and busy. "There's no next of kin listed. Are you a relative?"

Kerry felt the sudden hot press of tears as she thought of Patti's lack of family. "No, a friend."

Matt laid a hand over hers and nodded encouragement.

"Would we be allowed to arrange a cremation? Patti was a follower of the Spirit of Healing and—"

"I understand," the woman broke in. "You would have to get clearance from a judge. You'll need it today or in the morning at the latest. She's scheduled to be removed from the morgue for burial tomorrow."

"Oh—oh, I see," Kerry said.

"Ask what judge," Matt murmured, his temple touching hers as he listened in.

Kerry got the information, repeating it aloud while he wrote down names and numbers.

"That's all I can tell you," the secretary told her. In a kinder tone she added, "I'll make a note to hold things here until tomorrow afternoon. That's all the time I'll be able to give you without a court order."

"Thank you. I'm sure we can get something done by then. Thank you so very much." She hung up. "What's the judge's number?"

Matt held the notebook up so she could see.

After thirty minutes of being transferred from one person to another or put on hold with elevator music to listen to, Kerry found out the judge wouldn't be in his office until the following day.

"He has court in the morning starting at nine," she reported. "It's a long case and he'll be tied up all day."

"Let's think this through," Matt said. After a moment, he murmured, "I have an idea."

He pulled out his cell phone and flipped through the notebook. In less than a minute he dialed a number. He grimaced when he got an answering machine, but left his name and number.

Next he called Claude Pichante, Jason's father. Again he had to leave a message.

Matt muttered an expletive when he hung up. "If we don't hear from one of them in an hour, we'll go to Plan B," he told her.

Her spirits perked up. "What is Plan B?"

He gave her a wry grin. "We have an hour to figure it out. I thought we could start with Detective Rothberg."

"Good thinking," she said.

The hour ticked by. Matt talked to the detective in the interim but got no ideas from him. Just as Kerry gave up hope, Matt's cell phone rang.

"Matt Anderson," he said into the phone. "Claude, good of you to return my call."

He explained their problem to Claude Pichante while Kerry prayed he could be of help with the bureaucracy of local government.

After a brief conversation, Matt thanked the man and hung up. "He just finished a round of golf and is heading for the clubhouse for lunch. He saw a judge from Superior Court on the golf course earlier. He'll try to locate him and see if he can help us."

She laid a hand on his arm. "Oh, Matt, thank you. You are just wonderful—"

He leaned close, his breath fanning her lips as he spoke. "Keep looking at me like that and we'll end up spending the day in bed," he warned huskily.

She was so spellbound she couldn't look away.

"Ah, honey," he said on a low groan, "you make it hard to remember I'm a gentleman."

Kerry thought maybe she wanted him to forget, but she controlled the longing to ignore common sense— she was *not* going to lose her head during a one-week vacation—and pointed to the telephone to remind both of them of their goal.

"Would you like to explore the Quarter while we wait for his call?" she asked.

He let out a gusty sigh as if he'd gotten past a terrible temptation. "Sure."

They strolled along the busy streets and checked out the churches, museums and shops in the Vieux Carré for over two hours before heading back to the hotel and taking a break on her patio.

Kerry was beginning to feel despondent. Time was running out on the chance to give Patti a healing ceremony and lay her spirit to rest. It had probably been a hopeless and ridiculous idea from the start.

In fact, she was so sure it wasn't going to happen that she was startled when Matt's phone buzzed.

He grabbed it from his pocket and answered. "It's kind of you to take my call, your honor," he said after identifying himself.

He patiently went over the situation, then answered several questions. Kerry's name was mentioned as a friend of the deceased when Matt explained what she wanted to do and why.

After writing some info down, he thanked the judge and finally hung up. "We got it," he said.

"What?"

"The judge's okay. He's not the judge whose name you were given, but he can also give the permission we need. He's calling his office now. His legal assistant will cut the order and he'll stop by and sign it in about thirty minutes. The forms can be picked up by the crematorium staff so they can collect the remains. He gave me the number of one that's reliable and said we could use his name when we contacted them."

Kerry clutched his arm. "I'm so relieved. I'd almost given up."

Matt gave her a smile that warmed her heart. "I'll call now." In another minute he was speaking to the director of the crematorium. "Could you make it this afternoon?" he asked and explained the time crunch. "Thanks. That's a big relief to us. When can we get the, uh…"

Matt glanced at Kerry. She knew he was trying not to say "ashes" in front of her.

"Yes, an urn would be fine," Matt continued. "Does

it have a cover? Okay. Yes. After nine in the morning. Is a credit card okay? Good. We'll see you then." He hung up.

"How much is it going to cost?" she asked, worrying about her credit limit.

He told her. "We'll split it. I want to," he added when she started to protest that it was her idea.

A large warm hand touched her chin and brought her face up. "I can't stand it when you look so sad," Matt said.

Tears filled her eyes. She couldn't stop them. "I keep thinking of all that potential. Wasted. All that Patti could have been, gone. It was the same with my cousin. She was lovely and talented and a straight-A student. Patti seems to have been the same."

"I know."

"Apparently she was studying to be a healer under the old queen. I think she must have been a very caring person."

Her throat closed and she couldn't go on. Matt pushed his chair back and drew her into his arms, settling her in his lap. "Go ahead and cry," he whispered.

Kerry did. She laid her head on his shoulder and let the hot sad tears fall.

Matt didn't say a word, but simply held her, one hand rubbing her back until her tears were spent. In a few minutes, she sniffed and managed a laugh.

"How embarrassing," she said, trying for a light tone.

"How human," he corrected.

OFFICIAL OPINION POLL

Dear Reader,

Since you are a book enthusiast, we would like to know what you think.

Inside you will find a short Opinion Poll. Please participate in our poll by sharing your opinion on 3 subjects that are very important to all of us.

To thank you for your participation, we would like to send you your choice of **2 FREE BOOKS** and a **FREE GIFT!**

Please enjoy them with our compliments.

Sincerely,

Pam Powers

Editor

P.S. Don't forget to indicate which books you prefer so we can send your FREE gifts today!

What's your pleasure...

Romance?

Enjoy 2 FREE BOOKS that will fuel your imagination with intensely moving stories about life, love and relationships.

(OR)

Suspense?

Enjoy 2 FREE BOOKS that will thrill you with a spine-tingling blend of suspense and mystery.

Whichever category you select, your **2 FREE BOOKS** have a combined cover price of $11.98 or more in the U.S. and $13.98 or more in Canada.

Simply place the sticker next to your preferred choice of books, complete the poll on the right page and you'll automatically receive **2 FREE BOOKS** and a **FREE GIFT** with no obligation to purchase anything!

The tears threatened again. His smile was exquisitely tender. She held the emotion in check as she leaned her head against his arm and gazed up at his wonderful face.

"Kerry," he said.

He kissed her and it reawakened everything she'd experienced last night. He made her feel hunger, yes, but there was more.

Wonder and happiness filled her. The blood seemed to rush in a giddy stream through her body, and she felt almost light-headed.

She clasped his shoulders and held on as tightly as she could while the world disappeared in a hazy mist....

SHORTLY BEFORE DINNER, Kerry took a relaxing soak, then did her nails and hair. After dressing in slacks and a cotton sweater with a matching cardigan in case the evening got cool, she called her sister.

"Hey, Sharon," she said, recognizing the voice that answered on the third ring.

"Kerry!" her sister shrieked in her ear as if she'd been gone for years rather than three days. "Are you having a wonderful time? Have you met a divine man yet?"

Kerry laughed and answered the second question honestly. "Yes, I've met a divine man. I am having a good time, but there are complications."

"What kind of complications?"

"It's a long story, but first, how are the kids?"

"Very spotty," Sharon said and gave a long-suffering sigh. "The doctor said we were lucky. The vaccine, which doesn't always prevent chicken pox, at least made it a much lighter case. I'm grateful for that," she added sardonically. "I'm pretty sure Ryan and I couldn't handle a heavy case of scratching and whining. Oh, the kids also want to know when their wonderful, story-reading aunt is coming home. I told them 'never' if they continued to fight."

Kerry made sympathetic noises.

"Now get back to the complications," Sharon ordered. "And don't leave out the divine hunk part."

"Well, I guess I should start at the beginning." She began with lunch on Saturday and described meeting Patti, the waitress. Then she covered the voodoo museum and Queen Patrice and Madame Jolie, the python.

"Yuck," Sharon said. "I couldn't touch a snake, much less let it hang all over me. What if it had decided to give you a squeeze?"

"Well, it didn't. Hush, now, and let me finish."

With all her sister's interruptions, it took over an hour for Kerry to finally get to Matt.

"Matt Anderson," Sharon repeated. "Kerry Anderson doesn't sound bad."

"Sharon, puh-leeze. We just met." She sighed. "It does seem we've known each other a lot longer. I've never run across anyone that I liked half so much in such a short time. Isn't that odd?"

"No, it isn't. Have you gone to bed with him yet?"

"Well, I've thought of it," Kerry admitted. "A lot."

Sharon laughed like a maniac while Kerry winced.

"Live it up, big sister," Sharon advised. "How often do you get to go to someplace warm and romantic like New Orleans? Did you see on the news that we are enjoying a balmy twenty degrees and snow flurries?"

"Well, it's in the sixties here and *I'm* sizzling."

Sharon whooped with laughter again.

Kerry told her about the country club and the three glasses of wine and a cocktail. "Matt was a perfect gentleman and didn't take advantage. I must admit I'm not much of a lady. I want to drag him into my lair—uh, suite—each time I see him."

"Go for it!"

"You think I should?"

"Yes, I do. You're much too controlled. Lose your head—at least for a little while. Just don't forget protection."

"Yeah, like: Hi, Matt. My place or yours? Do you have condoms or shall I pick up a box? Uh-huh, I can see it now." Kerry's voice held more than a touch of cynicism.

"You're not blasé enough to carry that off," Sharon told her, "but you could relax and let nature take its course. Who knows? It could be the beginning of a happily-ever-after ending."

"I'd settle for happy-right-now and forget the ending."

Images flashed through her mind. Of Matt in black briefs with strong, muscular legs and lean hips. In jeans and a shirt, a sweater draped round his shoulders for the healing ceremony. In an expensive suit, quite at ease among the elite of the city and making her feel as lovely as any queen. The happiness she'd mentioned flooded her heart.

"Atta girl," Sharon said. "One more thing. I'm at my computer. Would you like me to see if I can get any info on the Ruoui family of Louisiana?"

"Yes. Matt and I are planning to find Patti's childhood home and scatter her ashes there. I think it's called Cordon Rouge. I hope that's the place of rest for her spirit— at least that's what the old voodoo queen suggested."

"Most of us look back on our childhoods as happy times. Hey, I got something on a Ruoui family near New Orleans." Sharon read the details. "A big wedding over thirty years ago. The bride was a debutante. If this is Patti's family, that must have been in the days when they still had money or pretended to."

"Great. Can you find anything that mentions Patti or Patrice Ruoui?"

"Oh-oh, I hear fighting in the family room," Sharon interrupted. "I have to go. I'll get back to you as soon as I can. Have fun, Kerry, and I mean it!"

After hanging up the phone, Kerry lingered in her room, her thoughts turning to Matt. She wondered if he had locked their adjoining door. If he hadn't and she opened it, what would he think?

She was tempted to take her sister's advice and have some fun on this trip. Oh, yes, she was tempted. What had years of being reserved gotten her but a bruised heart and intense loneliness. Besides, this was likely the only vacation of this kind that she would ever have.

Taking a liberating breath, she decided to go for it…if Matt was agreeable. Remembering the look in his eyes when he'd promised they would have another time, she was positive he was. Well, almost positive.

As she stood, the charm bracelet jingled merrily. She realized a ray of sunshine had found a slit in the sheer curtains over the window and shone on her arm. That must be the reason the bracelet suddenly felt so warm against her skin.

KERRY STOOD near Luc Carter's desk and admired a flower arrangement. She wanted to talk to the concierge about botanical gardens in the area since her grandmother, a gardening enthusiast, was sure to ask.

He was turned away from her and speaking in a low voice on a cell phone. She couldn't hear the words, but he sounded…angry.

"I can't…" he began, but she couldn't hear the rest. "The blackout did enough damage."

Kerry realized he must be speaking of the weekend's events at the lovely old hotel. The staff seemed so loyal to the Marchand family. She sighed and headed for her room to see if Matt had returned. The botanical garden could wait.

LUC STABBED THE BUTTON on his phone to end the call. He'd sensed someone waiting to see him, but no one was there when he turned around.

Things seemed to be growing out of control. He'd stolen a Wyeth painting from the hotel gallery to stir up trouble for the Marchand family, but he'd returned it before Sylvie, who ran the gallery, had alerted anyone. He figured he'd done his part to destroy the hotel's reputation by filling the generator's feed line with sugar. The timing of the blackout was a lucky break—his only one lately. He'd messed up several of the guest rooms to unnerve people, and his tactics had worked to a degree.

But it wasn't enough for Dan and Richard. They were pressuring him to do more. He was beginning to regret his involvement with the brothers. After working for them in Thailand, he knew their business ethics were questionable. They wanted to destroy the Hotel Marchand's reputation so they could buy it cheap, then flip it for a quick profit. Just as they'd done with previous properties.

Rubbing a hand across his forehead, he admitted that he wasn't sure anymore about hurting his aunt and her daughters. They didn't seem as bad as he'd thought they must be. But then it was his grandmother Celeste who was the real witch—the person responsible for his father's raw deal in life.

He threw himself into a comfortable armchair, glad no one wanted information or a booking for a fancy restaurant at the moment.

Forcing his reservations aside, he reminded himself that he'd laid his plans with care. Things were working out. All he had to do was keep a low profile, a cool head, and the hotel would sink....

MATT FELT ONLY a little guilt for not telling Kerry all he'd done earlier. At present, he was on his way to a review of a restaurant wine cellar, but he'd spent the last hour filling out forms at the crematorium and selecting an urn and cremation box.

There was no way he would put Kerry through that. He could tell she was still troubled by her cousin's suicide and Patti's lack of family.

Just thinking of Kerry brought a smile to his face and a surge in his pulse rate. And a desire to return to her as quickly as possible. With a grimace, he realized that wasn't going to be soon.

For the rest of the afternoon, he concentrated on his job. He and his host reviewed one of the most extensive wine lists he'd ever encountered in a restaurant. Both French and California wines were generously represented, but there was also a good selection from New York and Virginia, Australia and South Africa. They sampled twelve bottles, of which two were excellent, the rest fine as dinner wines.

When Matt finished nearly three hours later, his

impatience to return to the Hotel Marchand surprised him. Before he could analyze the feeling, he ran into another man as he left the restaurant.

"Jason," he said. "How are you?"

Jason Pichante stared at him in open hostility. "What the hell are you trying to pull?"

Matt studied the angry young man while suppressing his own aroused temper. "What's your problem?" he asked once he'd cooled down.

"You talked to my father this morning," Jason accused him. "He said you wanted permission to…"

Jason was overcome by emotion, but Matt didn't feel very sympathetic.

"…to collect Patti's…remains."

"Yes. She made friends with Kerry. Since there appears to be no next of kin, Kerry and I took over. The old voodoo queen, who was Patti's spiritual advisor, said we should have a cremation."

Jason stared at the pavement while Matt spoke. He could have been made of stone, Matt thought. He was that motionless.

When he still didn't speak, Matt continued, "We were also told to scatter her ashes in a place that would bring her rest." He paused. "Do you happen to know where that would be? A place where she was happy?"

The pupils of his eyes were so wide, Jason's irises looked black. Matt thought they reflected a bleakness within his soul. He felt a little sorry for the younger man.

"There was a place," Jason said in a voice so low Matt had to lean closer to hear. "I don't know if she would find peace there."

"Cordon Rouge?" Matt asked.

Jason's hand, which was fisted at his side, jerked at the name. "Yes. Her home...a long time ago."

"Do you know how to find it?"

A moment slipped by before Jason spoke. He gave Matt directions to a tiny town called Indigo out on Bayou Teche, southwest of New Orleans in Cajun country. "You can ask in town. They can direct you to the plantation. It's part of the national wetlands now, so it's public land."

"Thanks. I'll tell Kerry."

Jason nodded and started on down the street. He paused. "Are you going out there soon?"

"Tomorrow," Matt told him.

The younger man clenched his hand again, then he crossed the street, without another word.

As he watched Jason go, Matt noticed a branch of the bank that the Pichante family owned. He wondered if Jason worked for the family business.

Starting out once more, he quickly walked the few blocks to the hotel. His heart felt much lighter as he entered the courtyard from the alley. Odd, he thought, how you could meet someone and suddenly life seemed better...

He spotted Kerry seated at a table under an umbrella, talking to two women. He headed toward her.

"Hello," she said upon seeing him, her manner so full of welcome it was all he could do to keep from crushing her against him and holding her, just holding her.

Cool it, some saner part of him cautioned. While Kerry seemed the embodiment of all his dreams, he wasn't going to lose his head over any woman.

"Good afternoon," he said to all three women.

"You've met Charlotte," Kerry continued, "and this is her mother, Anne Marchand. I was just telling them about Patti's cremation and our plans for tomorrow."

Matt shook hands with the older woman, who was around sixty, he estimated, but looked younger and was in fact a very attractive woman. By contrast her daughter seemed tired and stressed, as if she hadn't slept well lately.

Since Saturday night, he was willing to bet. His gaze went to Kerry, who looked bright and alert and, okay, *wholesome* in slacks and a sweater that showed off her curves to perfection. It seemed to Matt she grew more beautiful each time he saw her.

"Join us," Kerry invited, smiling up at him.

He sat in the vacant chair between Kerry and Anne.

"I must tell you that I'm surprised at what you two are doing for that unfortunate young woman," Anne said, looking from one to the other. She shook her head. "You are living proof of the kindness of strangers."

A silence, tense with sadness, ensued. Kerry's eyes were moistened, Matt noticed.

"I stopped by the crematorium," he told her, his tone gentle. "Everything is going as planned."

She laid a hand on his arm, her eyes on him as if he'd done some heroic deed. "Thank you, Matt. That's a load off my mind." She turned to the two women. "We're going to find her former home and scatter her ashes there."

"The detective said she listed no next of kin at the restaurant where she worked," Charlotte mentioned.

"Kerry and I did some sleuthing and found out where she was from," Matt said. "There was once a family plantation." He turned to look at Kerry. "It's not far from Lafayette. If we leave between nine and ten in the morning, we should have plenty of time. I've arranged for a rental car."

Kerry pressed the heel of her hand to her forehead. "Oh, I didn't think about transportation and all that. Yes, let's leave early and get it over with."

"You two haven't had a vacation at all," Anne protested. "You're using your time to help others."

Charlotte nodded. "I agree. It so happens there have been a few cancellations since Saturday." She smiled at the couple. "Won't you stay another week as our guests? That seems only fair. Or if that isn't possible, then you must return another time and give us a chance to make your stay here as pleasant—and uneventful— as it should be."

"That's very kind of you," Kerry said. "I could stay over a couple of days. I didn't schedule any appointments until next Thursday in order to have a few days to settle in before I return to work. How about you?"

When she glanced at Matt, he nodded agreement. "I'll be writing an article based on my research in the city. I can do it here as well as in New York."

"Wonderful," Anne said, rising and wishing them all a good day.

Charlotte paused after her mother left them. "Please have dinner as our guests this evening. In fact, all your meals will be comped. I insist," she added when Matt and Kerry assured her they expected no such thing.

"Well," Matt said when he was alone with Kerry, "my publisher will be pleased. My expense account should be much lower than expected on this trip."

"What about the rental car?" she asked.

"That's a personal expense," he said, "something I want to do. With you."

Her eyes widened, then gleamed with pleasure. "Me, too," she said softly.

Matt's heart set off again. That old black magic of legend and song had them in its spell, it seemed.

Funny, but in this case, he didn't mind. Being attracted to Kerry was fine. As long as he didn't do anything stupid like think he was falling in love.

CHAPTER EIGHT

ON WEDNESDAY, Kerry and Matt were in the rental car and heading out of the city shortly before ten. In her lap she held a wooden urn carved with good *Ju-Ju* symbols and lightning bolts. The lightning must represent thunder, she assumed, which symbolized the Spirit of Healing.

She inhaled deeply and caught the fresh scent of Matt's shampoo and aftershave. Tingles rushed over her nerve endings. Odd, to be happy and sad at the same time.

Thinking of Patti reminded her of her beloved cousin, who had gone off alone to die. Presumably Patti's date—Kerry had a gut feeling it was Jason Pichante—had been with her when she died, but she thought the beautiful young woman had mostly lived a very lonely life.

"You're quiet," Matt said when they were out of town and on the highway.

"I thought most men were grateful for that," she teased, trying for a light tone.

"Not when I know it's because you're sad. Besides, I like it when you talk to me."

His voice was so deep, so warm, it added another ache to her heart. She would hate to leave New Orleans. And him.

Holding the seat belt out of the way, she turned so she could face him, one leg drawn up under her. His profile was endearing, his features strong. Maturity and responsibility rested easily on his broad shoulders. Glancing at the urn, she acknowledged he was a man who knew how to get things done. He had made this trip much easier for her in many ways.

"I do mourn Patti, but not in an acute way—more like for an old friend from years ago. I can't change anything that happened in her life, so I'll remember only that she was kind to me, a stranger in town who felt a little lost that first day. This may sound odd, but in a way she's given purpose to this trip, which I'd thought was a waste of time, although I couldn't tell my sister and friends that."

"But you don't feel that way anymore?"

Emotions too fleeting to be identified flashed through her. "No, not anymore." Her voice was unexpectedly shaky.

"I'm glad we met, even in these circumstances," he told her. He flicked her a glance. "Very glad."

She nodded.

Matt drove west on the interstate, then turned south on a road that would take them to New Iberia, the heart of Cajun country. A lot of the land southwest of New Orleans was salt marsh. At times the route was on a raised causeway surrounded by reeds that grew thick in shallow basins of water.

The ravages of the terrible hurricane season the year before last were still visible in uprooted trees and houses crushed by the wind and water. Many residents had obviously decided not to return.

"Look, in that tree." She whispered, although the beautiful white birds couldn't hear her.

"Cranes," he said.

Other long-legged birds stood in the water, dipping to grab a tempting morsel every now and then. Wispy clouds floated overhead.

"The clouds are thicker than when we first set out," she said.

"The weatherman said there would be no rain this week."

"Yeah, and in Minnesota he forecast possible snow flurries and those flurries are now over a foot deep."

They laughed together, and the conversation remained lighthearted until they reached St. Martinville. Matt slowed, then pulled into a parking space. "There's something here I thought you might like to see."

She followed him without question, something she wouldn't normally have done. She would have wanted to know why they'd stopped and what they were going to see.

Trust, she thought as he took her hand and led her down the street. She trusted this man. The insight caused a warm glow inside her.

"Oh," she said when he stopped in front of a lovely statue of a woman, seated, a long cloak draping her shoulders and back. The base the statue sat upon was a crypt, Kerry realized, an above-ground vault like those at the cemetery in New Orleans.

"Evangeline," she said, reading the statue's inscription.

"She was immortalized in Longfellow's poem as the symbol of a love that never faltered," Matt murmured.

"And was never fulfilled," she whispered. "When she found Gabriel after years of searching, he'd married someone else and gone on with his life."

She stared up at Matt, anguish clutching her heart. What if she'd never met this man? What if they parted next week and never saw each other again?

A worried frown lined his brow. "Perhaps I shouldn't have brought you here. You and your tender heart," he added, his eyes filled with…tenderness? concern? regret? Did he regret meeting her?

She swallowed hard. "No, no. It was thoughtful of you. I would have been disappointed if I'd realized we were so close and I'd missed it."

He glanced at his watch. "It's after twelve. Shall we go?"

They returned to the car and soon arrived at a small bayou town called Indigo.

"Indigo is a plant, isn't it?" she asked.

"Yes. It was grown commercially in the area for blue dye. I don't know if it still is."

The town was built on a graceful curve of road that followed the bayou, which Kerry could see beyond the town "square," which was really a lawn.

Matt surprised her with a picnic lunch packed by the Hotel Marchand. Another indication of his thoughtfulness, she noted. They ate on the grassy grounds of the town square.

"How did you know picnics were one of my favorite things?" she demanded, opening a covered plastic plate that was filled with roasted chicken bites, mandarin orange slices and crisp noodles on a bed of mixed greens.

He handed her a container of dressing and a napkin and fork, then opened the bottle of sparkling rosé that was included. "Because I like them, too," he said, giving her a quick perusal that made her head feel as if she'd already had a couple of glasses of wine. "I've noticed we like a lot of the same things."

She nodded and wondered if her eyes were as sparkly as she felt inside. "Look at that building at the head of the square," she said, to distract her disquieting thoughts. "It's pretty fancy."

"We'll go over after we eat and check it out."

Forty minutes later they strolled across the lawn and paused in front of the ornate building. It was an antique shop, but a brochure explained that it had once been an opera house, a gift from a local plantation owner to his wife.

"That was wonderful of him."

Matt ruffled her bangs. "Yeah. Men like to do things for the women they love."

A warm, happy glow spread over Kerry, but ever cautious, she tamped it down. "We'd better go if we expect to get back to the city before dark."

"What happens then?" Matt questioned wryly. "Do we turn into vampires?"

"Or werewolves," Kerry said crisply. She got into the rental vehicle without waiting for his help and had her seat belt fastened by the time he was inside.

She was, she felt, in danger of wearing her heart on her sleeve. The statue, then the opera house, touched her in ways she couldn't explain, except that both represented a deep, abiding love. And then there was Matt's thoughtfulness. It made her want to wrap herself around him and never let go.

Taking a deep breath, she vowed not to embarrass either of them by assuming too much. Instead she commented on the old buildings and the charm of the countryside, plus the pleasure of being in Cajun country, which she'd read about before leaving White Bear Lake.

Matt, she noticed, had a note in his hand. He checked it, then made a turn onto a dusty road so narrow she hoped they didn't meet another car. He took a left when the road split, then another later on.

"Hmm, see if you can figure out our next turn," he said, passing the directions to her.

"Who told you how to get here?"

"Jason Pichante. I saw him yesterday. I got the name of the town from him and directions to the plantation from the parish maps."

"Good work." She hesitated. "There seemed to be so much anger in Jason when we met him at the warehouse."

"There still is. I think it's directed as much at himself as his father."

"Because he abandoned Patti? I think he was the date she was with, don't you?"

Matt shrugged. "Maybe. We seem to have reached a dead end. Did I miss a turn?"

She read over the directions. "No, we did everything written here. Maybe we turned too soon at some point."

"Or too late," Matt added with a frown.

"There's a house up that lane. I can see it through the trees. That may be the place."

Matt backed up and turned into a weed-choked lane. A small house sat in the middle of a tidy, flower-strewn yard. "Not exactly a plantation," he said.

A woman came outside and observed them as they climbed out and walked up a brick path to the front porch. The small home was built high off the damp ground.

Matt introduced Kerry and himself and explained that they were lost. "Cordon Rouge is…was the name of the place we're looking for," he finished. "It's part of a preserve now, I understand."

"It's difficult to get to," the woman said. "The road has not been maintained."

Tall and thin, she had skin the color of coffee laced with cream. Her eyes were light green, like those of a kitten Kerry's grandmother had raised. She wore a long black skirt with a starched and ironed long-sleeved white blouse.

Like the old voodoo queen, her age was indeterminate. Kerry guessed she must be in her eighties or nineties.

"Why do you wish to go there?" she asked.

Matt and Kerry glanced at each other before he said, "It's a favor for a friend."

"A young woman?" she asked.

The hair stirred on Kerry's neck as Matt nodded.

"Come," she now said, "and sit. You've had a long trip and will need something refreshing." She disappeared inside the house.

Kerry glanced up at Matt. He shrugged and took her arm, guiding her to a swing attached to the rafters of the porch. When the woman reappeared, he got to his feet and opened the screened door for her.

She served them tall glasses of iced tea with sprigs of mint on top and passed a plate of pecan cookies. After setting the tray on a low table and taking a seat in a cane-bottomed rocking chair, she studied them with those all-seeing eyes.

"What has happened to Patti?" the woman asked quietly.

Kerry actually gasped aloud.

Matt bowed his head slightly in acknowledgement of the woman's insight. "She died."

"What was the cause?"

Matt explained about the reaction to the love potion.

The woman said nothing, and the silence seemed electric with tension. Kerry shivered although the day was warm. At last the old woman made the sign of the cross, her gaze on the horizon as if she saw things they couldn't. "Then she didn't take her own life. I thank the good Lord."

"You knew her personally?" Matt asked.

"She and her father and grandfather. I am Atta. I was the housekeeper when Patrick Ruoui committed suicide. After setting fire to the house and barn, he stood by the bayou and shot himself in the head. I have never understood how he could be so selfish."

"Selfish?" Kerry questioned.

"Selfish," Atta stated, "to leave a grieving child behind. Patti's mother had died the year before. The girl needed him more than ever. The shame of it," she added sternly.

"He was losing the plantation," Matt said.

The wisdom of the ages seemed to reside in Atta's eyes as she gazed at him. "There was no plantation."

"Patti said Cordon Rouge was her home," Kerry told her.

"No, no. That was the old place. I was born there. It was taken by the state for back taxes and became a nature preserve some seventy years ago, all but this bit of land and my house. Patti's great-grandfather deeded this to my mother. Patti and her parents had another, smaller place near here, land that had once bordered the original plantation. It was bought and deeded to Patrick's father before the grandfather lost the plantation."

Kerry realized that the image she'd had of Patti living in a grand, but time-worn plantation in genteel poverty was totally wrong. "So it was a lie," she murmured, "the plantation and the life…."

"Perhaps," Atta said. "Who knows what is in the mind of another?" She gestured toward the charm bracelet. "You wear the three bones. Do you not know what they mean?"

"No."

"They represent three worlds, or manifestations. The material world—" she indicated everything they could see with a sweeping embrace of her arms "—the world we each create in our own minds and the spiritual world of which we know little."

Kerry thought of Patti's spirit. Where should she put Patti's ashes so that her troubled soul would find peace? "Can you tell us how to find Patti's home, the place she lived before her parents died?"

Atta nodded. "It was a cotton farm. On good bottom land, too. But Patrick wasn't a farmer or a businessman, either. He had dreams of returning to the glory of the old days. He put those dreams into Patti. It was never to be."

The finality of the statement dropped like a heavy rock within Kerry. She felt a sharp tug of sorrow. How must Patti have felt when her father shot himself?

"What happened after the death of Patrick Ruoui?" Matt asked.

Atta turned her probing gaze from Kerry to Matt. "After the house was closed, I went to work at the aunt's home—"

"Patti's aunt? The one she lived with?"

"Yes." The old woman glanced back at her. "It was a hard time for the girl. She wasn't wanted."

Kerry nodded, unable to look away from the anger in Atta's eyes. She touched her bracelet, found the cross that had been blessed and held on to it.

"The aunt was weak and the uncle was cruel," Atta said. Her voice became fierce. "That fine, rich house was no place for a child of any kind."

Kerry felt Matt's hand on hers, comforting and re-assuring.

"But Patti was special," Atta told them, her voice softening. "She had a good soul, an old one. She sur-vived. When she left for New Orleans and the college, I knew she would never return."

"And she didn't," Kerry concluded.

"Tell me of her death," the old woman commanded. Her voice was quieter now, like the sound of the wind through the moss that draped the trees.

Matt told her of finding Patti in his room on Twelfth

Night, of the healing ceremony and the old voodoo queen.

Atta closed her eyes and rocked slowly back and forth. "It will change your lives, this tragedy," she finally said.

Follow the shining path...

The words hummed through Kerry as she clung to Matt's hand. Her very soul felt in tumult, and the sensation spread through her, urgent and almost frightening in its intensity.

"Kerry and I did the cleansing rite," Matt said. "A cremation. We want to put her ashes in a place where she was once happy. That's why we were looking for the plantation."

"The marsh has reclaimed it."

"Perhaps we should go to the other place, the cotton farm," he said.

Atta stared at them, obviously troubled. She finally nodded. "I wouldn't have thought so, but perhaps you are right. You have been entrusted by the spirits with this deed, so only you can know for certain. But be sure before you spread the ashes. The ritual must be performed correctly for her spirit to find its rest." She looked at Kerry. "You must do it. You will know..."

Her voice trailed off but her gaze remained fixed on Kerry. The old woman nodded again, as if satisfied that Kerry was the chosen one for this task.

Almost without realizing it, Kerry nodded, accepting the quest as hers. "How do we find this other place?"

Atta gave them directions that would take them back to the gravel road and farther down the track. They were told that no one went there anymore, so the road would be overgrown by weeds, but they could get through.

They thanked Atta and started down the steps. "By the way," Matt said, "if we wanted to find Cordon Rouge or whatever is left of it, where would we look?"

"You can find the ruins," Atta said, "if you follow the carriage road to the house."

She indicated the lane they'd arrived on. Kerry realized it continued past the cottage and into the cypress bog beyond...to Cordon Rouge.

MATT KEPT AN EYE on the sky as he carefully navigated the long-unused road to the old cotton farm. The white-layered clouds of the morning had built into dark thunderheads.

He was thankful the farmhouse where Patti was born was no more than a mile from the cottage, but it took twenty minutes to get there. Weeds hit the front grill of the rental car with a steady thump. In places the road was so boggy, he'd driven as close to an old fence as possible to keep from getting stuck.

"Here it is," he announced as they came to the end of the road. When he got out of the car, he rotated his shoulders, trying to relieve the tension that had collected between his shoulder blades.

Glancing at Kerry's pale face, he decided it had

been a mistake to bring her here. But if he hadn't, he knew she would have somehow made it here on her own. He exhaled a deep breath and took her arm as they met in front of the vehicle.

"It's beautiful," she said, "but also wild and lonely."

He studied the burnt remains of the house. It had been a rather modest two-story with chimneys bracketing each end. Those and the foundation were all that could be identified. Vines had grown over everything else.

She gestured toward the backyard. "There would have been a garden, don't you think?"

Following Kerry, he helped search for signs of a garden or something recognizable from the farm.

Nothing.

An eerie sensation slid along his neck. The place felt lifeless, as if its soul had long departed.

He shook his head slightly, negating the notion. He was letting all this voodoo business get to him.

Beyond the house, the ruins of a barn and some tumbledown fences, the land had reverted to nature. Wild rice grew along the bayou, and the cypress trees were draped in Spanish moss. Waist-high weeds discouraged wandering about.

"Watch those thistles," he cautioned, pulling Kerry a bit closer with an arm around her shoulders.

"They look vicious." She leaned her head against him as they stopped at the end of a broken brick path. There was no gate, but a fence indicated the area had once been enclosed.

"Perhaps this was a garden once," he told her.

She nodded. Glancing back at the house, then over the backyard again, she sighed. "This isn't the place. I can't leave Patti...her ashes...here. It isn't her spiritual home."

Matt refrained from questioning her, knowing that logic didn't apply in this case, only Kerry's instincts. "Then we'll find another place."

She looked up at him, her face solemn. "Thank you, Matt, for accepting something that I don't really understand. It's just that I feel this isn't the right place."

"I know." His voice resonated with the desire to caress and comfort her.

He'd been close to his sister—growing up, they'd had only each other in many ways—but he'd never been so in tune with another person. He seemed to know instinctively what Kerry was feeling, as if their spirits were joined.

"Kerry," he murmured. "Sweetheart."

He kissed her then, and she wound her arms around his neck, returning the embrace with equal passion. When he lifted her off her feet, she swung her legs around his hips, making a snug fit against him. He groaned as the kiss became more intense, wilder, almost savage as their bodies demanded more.

Her mouth was nectar, a magic potion that fulfilled all the youthful dreams he'd ever had of finding *the* woman for him. He hadn't believed in those dreams for a long time, but now, each and every one of them seemed within reach.

He caressed her slender back, along her hips, following the curve of her slacks until he reached the place where the most pleasure dwelt for her. She gasped when he caressed her through the taut material and felt her legs tighten around him.

"Matt," she said on a shaky breath.

"Yeah, me, too," he agreed with a chuckle, his mind hazy with desire and a happiness he hadn't known in years. He kissed her again.

Hearing a rumble, he first thought it came from them, the voice of their passion, but then he realized it was thunder. He reluctantly raised his head.

"A storm," he said. "We'd better get out of here fast."

Another bolt split the sky right over their heads, followed by a deafening blast. Setting her on her feet, he took her hand just as a drop of rain hit his cheek. "Let's run for it."

Laughing and breathless, they made it to the car just as the sky opened up and spilled a torrent of water down on the old cotton farm. He started the car, backed, then headed along the road once more.

"I hope we can get out," Kerry said. "This area is pretty swampy."

"I can think of worse things than being stranded here overnight. Well, being alone would be worse, a lot worse," he added. He gave her a sexy glance that made her laugh.

Smiling, he concentrated on getting them out of

the low bayou land before it flooded. He flicked the headlights onto bright. When they passed the carriage lane, he couldn't spot Atta's cottage in the woods through the heavy curtain of rain.

Well over an hour later, they arrived at the tiny town. He rotated his shoulders, glad to be back in civilization. In truth, he had been worried about getting stuck out in the wilds in an area he wasn't familiar with. Here in town, they were on higher ground, so there was less chance of flooding.

"The rain is so heavy," Kerry murmured. "Perhaps we should…"

He saw her press her lips together as if to halt the flow of words. A jolt of pure lust speared through him. "Stop for the night?" he finished for her.

"But then, we're only a couple of hours from New Orleans," she reasoned aloud. "And the main roads will be better as we get closer to the city."

She didn't sound convinced, and Matt realized she didn't want to go on any more than he did, a fact that filled him with exaltation. "I'm ready for a break. I noticed a restaurant and inn in St. Martinville, close to the statue of Evangeline. Shall we check it out?"

He realized he was practically holding his breath as he waited for her answer.

She didn't hesitate. "That would be wonderful."

CHAPTER NINE

TRAFFIC WAS LIGHT when Kerry and Matt returned to St. Martinville. Using his jacket as a cover, they dashed up the steps to the inn Matt had mentioned. The building was a two-story Victorian, old-fashioned in design but newly renovated. It had obviously been rebuilt after Hurricane Katrina had swept through.

The large front room had windows on three sides and opened onto a wraparound screened porch with ferns and potted plants. An assortment of tables, cushioned chairs and wicker settees provided lots of seating both inside and on the porch.

"This is charming," Kerry said, pausing to brush off droplets of rain on the porch. "I hope we don't look suspicious, not having any luggage."

"You mean people might think we're having an assignation or something?" Matt asked, lowering his voice to a dramatic whisper, then spoiling the effect by grinning.

"Or something," she agreed drolly. She waved toward the leaded glass door through which she could see several couples seated at tables and enjoying the evening meal. "Lead on. I'll follow you."

He clasped her hand and tucked it into the crook of his elbow. "We'll go together."

The woman at the registration desk informed them that the inn did indeed have available accommodations. "It's a miserable night to be out, isn't it?" she added sympathetically.

"The roads are treacherous," Matt said, "which is why we decided to stop rather than try to make it back to New Orleans tonight." He turned to Kerry. "I wonder if we should let the night manager at the Hotel Marchand know that we won't be in?"

"That's a good idea, just in case Charlotte or someone asks about us. Although I don't know why anyone would."

"I would be glad to call for you," the B and B owner, Margaret Beaulieu, told them. "I went to school with Anne Marchand, so I know the family." She placed a form on the counter in front of Matt. "Would you prefer two queen-size beds or a king suite?"

Matt glanced at Kerry. Her eyes must have told him everything he needed to know. "The king would be fine," he told the woman and proceeded to fill out the form, giving his name and address and adding her name as his guest.

Her skin prickled at the thought of being listed as Kerry Anderson, spouse.

No, no, she ordered the sentimental part of her that wanted to read more into her and Matt's involvement than truly existed. This was a…a vacation fling.

It was the drama of the past few days that made each moment more important and each emotion more intense than it actually was, would it even be wise to become more deeply involved?

But what had waiting, being cautious, gotten her but a bruised heart? A four-year engagement should have clued her in that she and her fiancé were *not* meant for each other.

Seize the moment. That was her new motto. She glanced at Matt. At least where this man was concerned, it was. She gave him a warm smile when he finished the form and handed it, along with his credit card, to their hostess.

The heated look he returned made her feel weak in the knees. What would he think if she grabbed him here in the lobby and kissed him until they were senseless?

She was still laughing at the thought of Matt's reaction when they went up the staircase and along the hall to the last room. Matt unlocked the door, pushed her gently inside then closed the door and lifted her onto an intricately carved footstool placed in front of a wing chair.

"Woman," he said on a low growl, then *he* kissed *her* until they were both senseless.

It was heavenly.

Kerry pressed herself against him until they touched everywhere, until it seemed as if they would merge into one. The added height allowed her to experience his body in a whole new way.

When she felt his thigh press between hers, his erection hard and hot, she didn't hesitate, but opened to him. He lifted one foot to the stool so that her right leg rested over his thigh, heightening the sensation.

"Matt," she whispered when he let her up for air. He nibbled her neck with little love bites, then moved intimately against her. Kerry nearly fainted with pleasure.

"Being with you all day has made me…"

She held her breath as she waited to hear what word he would use to describe the oh, so evident hunger.

"…edgy," he concluded, a hint of laughter in his deep, husky voice.

She nodded in understanding. "I can't decide whether I'm going to explode or swoon, but something has to happen…soon!"

"No way you're going to faint on me," he stated firmly, his lips exploring the corner of her mouth while his hands did wonderful things to her body.

Delight bubbled in her, a frothing pool of lust and wonder and other feelings she hadn't experienced since she was maybe sixteen years old and madly in love with her science teacher, who was newly out of college.

"My legs are getting weak," she warned.

He raised his head and sucked in a deep breath. "This is just the warm-up. We should have dinner before the dining room closes, but then we'll have all the time in the world…all the time." His wicked drawl made her laugh, mitigating the disappointment she felt at not seeing the moment through to its tantalizing fulfillment.

He sighed loudly, grinned and let her go. "We'd better comb our hair before we go down."

They freshened up, then sedately walked down the stairs and joined the other three couples in the dining room. A fire blazed in the fireplace, taking the chill off the evening. A teenage girl, who told them she was the granddaughter of the owner, seated them at a cozy table for two next to a window.

"I like this," Kerry said of the secluded space between the hearth and the wall of windows. Potted plants separated most of the tables, ensuring privacy.

Matt looked only at her. "Me, too."

Their eyes locked. Kerry couldn't look away. It seemed astonishing…to feel this way…to know this terrible achy sense of anticipation…to want to touch this wonderful man, to tease out the journey until the moment their hunger would be sated…

Their waitress returned with glasses of water and a basket of rolls, bringing them back to the reality of the dining room.

They each chose a different seafood entrée, and Kerry ordered a salad and Matt a gumbo to start. He selected a rosé wine to go with their dinner.

"It's a sparkling, fruity wine. I think you'll like it." When it arrived, he held his glass toward her. "To our quest."

"The quest," she echoed. She clicked her glass against his and took a sip. "Mmm, it is good. What's the difference between sparkling wine and champagne?" she asked.

"Champagne comes from the Champagne region of France. The rest of the world produces sparkling wine. The French have tried to protect the name, but it's a losing battle."

His eyes seemed to darken as he leaned closer across the small table. Kerry swallowed as words dried in her mouth and refused to be uttered.

"I'll educate you in wines later," he promised. "Now I want to know everything about you. Tell me your earliest childhood memory, good or bad."

Kerry considered a moment. "Well, I once got very angry with my mother over something I no longer remember, but I do recall skipping down the road, heading for my grandmother's house and perhaps some cookies and sympathy, and shouting the worst word I knew."

"Would that be a four-letter word?" he asked.

She nodded and tried to look contrite.

He chuckled. "Did anyone hear you?"

"My sister told on me, and I was grounded for a month. However, being the magnanimous person that I am, I forgave her on her twenty-first birthday, and we're good friends now."

His laughter did sweet things to her insides, and every sense seemed heightened by his nearness. The salad with its spicy dressing, the gumbo, the sea bass and the blackened sunfish all tasted sublime. The hot berry tart with melted cheese, which they shared, was the best dessert she'd ever had.

Because of him, some part of her whispered.

Yes, her heart answered happily.

She refused to worry about the consequences of falling too quickly and deeply for this man. This would be like a summer fling, and she wouldn't expect more.

Over coffee, he asked about her plans for their quest. "The housekeeper said you would know what to do. Any ideas?"

Mellow and introspective now, she nodded. "I'm thinking of sprinkling her ashes in the Mississippi and letting the current deposit them wherever it will. Is that illegal?"

"I don't know. I've thought of that, too. Or perhaps in the bayou."

"Bayou Rouge? I'm not sure she was happy there. My sister researched the Ruoui family on the Internet. She called and told me Patti's aunt and uncle live next to it." Kerry stopped and frowned.

"What?" Matt asked.

"Since Patti listed no next of kin and apparently cut herself off from them completely, do you think they were contacted about her death and…and refused to take responsibility for the burial?"

"I wondered about that."

"From what Atta said, they weren't loving relatives. Why did they dislike her so?" Kerry asked, her expression earnest.

"There was a land dispute between Patti's father and her aunt. I assume the aunt was angry that her brother inherited the property."

"But he lost the farm anyway."

"Yes. I suppose he couldn't face an I-told-you-so from them. When I was looking for directions at the county clerk's office, I found out the aunt and her husband bought the farm back by paying the outstanding taxes, so Patti got nothing from what should have been her inheritance."

"So why aren't they farming it?" Kerry asked, indignant.

Matt shrugged.

After a moment, Kerry added, "Patti seemed like a caring person, in spite of her family's behavior. As Atta said—she had a good soul."

Matt studied Kerry. He could hear the sadness and regret in her voice for the young woman whose life had been so hard. He thought *her* soul was pretty darned nice, too.

Wholesome, he mused, applying his favorite description, unable to stop gazing at her as if she were a rare and perfect piece of porcelain. Being around Kerry made him appreciate life in a way he hadn't in years.

"But she never found herself," Kerry continued. "Her life was full of possibilities, but she never had the chance to explore them. I hope she at least found love with Jason Pichante."

Matt felt both anger and pity for the young man who had wanted Patti but had denied that love.

"Do you think he loved her?"

He wouldn't lie to Kerry. "I think he did, but not enough to defy his father for her, or give up his privileged life and make a new one with Patti."

"He'll regret his cowardliness all his life."

Kerry gazed into the fire as if looking into the future, sure of what she saw there. Matt laid his hand over hers, bringing her back to the present and to him.

"Are you ready to go upstairs?" he asked.

Her smile was everything he could have asked for, and it was only for him. He recalled he had a couple of things of Patti's, to give her. But those could wait for the morning. The night was his....

KERRY THOUGHT her heart was going to thump its way right out of her chest as they entered the pleasant suite with the king-size bed.

The covers were turned back, and there were chocolate mints on the marble-topped tables on each side of the bed. The cozy ambiance of the room was enhanced by the lamps on each table. They were ornately painted with pink roses on their fat globes and could be turned down to a soft night-light.

Kerry took in everything, including the old-fashioned claw-footed tub in the bathroom. Interesting images came to mind. "This is so charming. I'm thinking of relaxing in the tub—" She stopped abruptly. "Actually," she admitted with a slightly shaky laugh, "relaxing isn't exactly what I have in mind."

"I think that's an excellent idea," he agreed, laying his hands on her shoulders. "It's fun, becoming new lovers, but it's also rather nerve-racking, isn't it?"

She relaxed with a sigh. "So you feel the tension, too?" she asked, glad she wasn't the only one with a slight case of nerves.

With a finger under her chin, he tipped her face up so he could gaze straight into her eyes. "Not the same way you probably do. I want you to know that all you have to do is say *stop* or *slow down* and that's what will happen. Everything we do will be mutually satisfying or we won't do it. Got that?"

She nodded. Then she threw her arms around him and squeezed as hard as she could. "Matt," she whispered, "I want everything!"

"Me, too, sweetheart," he assured her. Swinging her slender form into his arms, he carried her to the bed and with a playful grin dropped her onto its comfortable expanse.

Going into the bathroom, he turned the spigots on full and checked the water temperature before returning to Kerry.

She'd kicked off her shoes and propped several pillows behind her back while he was gone. Sitting beside her, he began unfastening the pearl buttons on the green silky blouse, something he'd envisioned doing many times that day.

When he'd finished, he slipped it off her shoulders and down her arms, delighting in the smoothness of her skin. A beige bra in a light-and-dark zebra pattern amused him for a moment before he stripped it from her.

"Ah, Kerry," he said. "You are incredibly beautiful."

The temptation was too great. He bent to her lovely breasts, the tips already contracted.

To him, she seemed small and delicate, but when she pulled him closer to her, he was reminded of the lithe strength in her, the need that matched his. He caressed up and down her smooth torso until he could stand it no longer.

"I have to see all of you," he said, moving slightly away from her, which brought a little cry of protest. He heard the sounds of running water. "Whoops."

After removing several packets from his jacket, he took them to the bathroom, quickly checked the bath water, then returned to the bed. He unfastened her slacks and laid them with her blouse and underwear on a padded chair.

"Don't move," he warned as he stripped out of his own clothing and tossed it onto the chair. There was no way he could disguise his desire for her when he turned around.

He saw her eyes sweep over him, then she smiled and held up her hands, inviting him back into her embrace. Scooping her into his own arms, he headed for the tub.

"Your bath awaits, madam," he intoned before carefully lowering her into the water.

"Mmm, this is wonderful."

"So are you," he said.

"Are you coming in?"

He hesitated. "Do you want me to?"

"Very much," she teased, her eyes darkening. "Very, *very* much."

As Matt joined her in the mammoth bathtub, the water rose perilously close to the top.

He leaned past her and opened the drain to lower the level a few inches, then added a bit more hot water. When he lifted her, she laid her hands on his shoulders, and he reclined against the slanted end, then settled her on top of him, her back to his chest.

"I want to kiss you," she demanded, not at all pleased with this arrangement. She expected equal access.

"If you cooperate, your every wish shall be granted," he murmured as if he were a genie she'd released from a bottle.

She schooled the impatience and enjoyed their sensuous play. Matt was determined to drive her crazy, and she was willing to let him. She'd get her chance at sweet revenge.

"Consider me your love slave," he finished on a sexy teasing whisper that tickled the hair at her temple.

He placed her head against his shoulder so her face was even with his, then he kissed her.

The playfulness disappeared when their lips met. The intensity was explosive and immediate. Never, Kerry thought just before her mind went hazy, could she have imagined passion to be so all-consuming. There was nothing else but *this*, the currents that flowed between them, in the entire world.

Matt had never felt so alive. The sensation of her skin against his was mind-blowing. When she moved slightly, her firm buttocks slid against him intimately, and he felt sure he was going to lose it right then. He tried to think of ice and snow, but all he felt was hot, intense need.

In this position, he was free to explore her without worrying about his weight on her. He took thorough advantage, sliding his hands over her perfect breasts, the plump nipples a rosy pink. They swelled into hard little beads as he stroked them.

Still holding her breast with one hand, he glided the other hand down to the juncture of her legs. From his position, he had a clear view of her body—the tiny mole close to her belly button, a thin white scar on her left knee, which she'd bent and rested against the side of the tub.

Mmm, he liked that position.

He changed hands, stroking the tiny patch of brown curls at the apex of her thighs, a slightly darker shade of brown than her hair, and heard her quickly drawn breath.

When he delved further, she buried her face against his neck, one hand clutching the side of the tub while the other caressed his hip.

"Matt," she said in a voice filled with desire.

He ravished her mouth, taking special delight in the fact that she was just as demanding as he was. His hands kept up their dual caresses, and when she writhed against him in need, he had to grit his teeth to keep from claiming all of her right then.

But he wanted more for them. He wanted them to reach heights neither had climbed before. He wanted to experience the full possibility that could be unleashed by the desire flaming between them. He wanted…everything.

Kerry couldn't stop the little moans and cries that demanded completion. He was driving her mad!

Yet she wanted more than this insane coupling in the bathtub, as fun and exciting as it was. "Matt," she whispered. "The bed…let's go to bed," she managed to gasp when his fingers delved into her, causing her to move instinctively against him.

"In a minute," he told her.

With expert care, he turned her, and cupping the back of her head, he kissed her until she was breathless. Opening her legs, she trapped his erection between her thighs and squeezed.

This time it was Matt who groaned and moved against her. He released her lips and gazed into her eyes, then helped her out of the cooling water and wrapped a towel around them. Bringing a foil packet, he guided her back to the bed, swept the covers out of the way and settled her on the sheets.

He took care of protection before joining her. "This is going to be bliss," he told her, his mood playful once more, but his eyes, oh, his eyes...

She wondered if anyone had ever drowned in eyes so blue, so filled with promises as they merged into one.

His trusts were deep and hard, and she was caught in a tide of swirling passion that lifted her higher and higher. She called out his name and clung to him as she was tossed to a far shore.

"Kerry, sweetheart," she heard him gasp just before he joined her in that distant place.

A long time later, sated and experiencing the most profound peace she'd ever known, she said sleepily, "You were right. It was bliss. I've never experienced anything half so wonderful."

A few minutes later, she felt him stir and lift away from her. She didn't want to give up the closeness, the perfection of this moment.

"I'll be back," he promised.

She heard him go into the bathroom. In less than two minutes he returned to her, and she was snug in his arms once more. He lay on his side, with one thigh over hers, his head resting on the mounded pillows.

With her eyes closed, she felt his fingers touch her face, roam down her neck and follow her collarbone to her shoulder, then back to her throat. Against her side, his chest rose and fell in a deep breath.

An impractical wish arose in her as she contemplated a life in which they could hold this moment forever. It was a ridiculous idea. They had less than a week left.

They made love once again, then lay propped against the pillows, listening to the wind and rain.

"Do you know what Dom Perignon said to his fellow monks when he found their white wine had undergone a second fermentation in the bottle and thus discovered champagne?" Matt asked her.

She opened her eyes and gazed into his. What an odd question, she thought. "No. What did he say?" she asked, not sure what to expect.

"'Brothers, I have drunk the stars.'" He touched her lips with one finger. "And so have I."

CHAPTER TEN

KERRY FELT as bright and refreshed as the land appeared after the storm. She and Matt were on their way back to the city after a leisurely breakfast, then a passionate interlude in which they discovered the fascinating possibilities in an old-fashioned tub with a shower curtain encircling them.

As they left the heart of Cajun country and the statue of Evangeline, Kerry felt almost wistful, as if she was leaving a part of herself here. She studied Matt and wondered if he felt the same.

He glanced at her. "What?"

"How do you always know when I have a question or something I want to discuss?"

A slow smile curved his lips. "Maybe we're soul mates."

"Yeah, yeah," she said, pretending skepticism but feeling a tiny pang at the idea.

"So what's your question?"

"I'm wondering if we should talk to Ashley or some of the other workers on the float for some suggestions about Patti. Maybe they know a place where her soul would be at rest."

"I might have a clue," he said, surprising her. "The medical examiner's secretary gave me a packet. It's in the inside breast pocket of my jacket. I was going to ask you if we should leave it with the ashes."

"What is it?"

"Apparently some stuff Patti had with her the night she died."

A flicker of dread went through Kerry. She looked into the back and spotted his sport coat. "Your jacket may never recover from the storm and being damp all night. We should have hung it in the closet."

"The cleaners can fix it," he assured her, giving her a quick smile before taking the off-ramp to the street that would lead to the hotel.

It seemed like a million years since their departure yesterday, Kerry thought. So much had happened that time seemed to have expanded into years rather than hours.

She withdrew the manila envelope from Matt's pocket and opened it.

Inside she found a tiny purse with a long chain, a pair of inexpensive carnival earrings and the gold ring with the intricate love knot. The purse contained a driver's license, a twenty-dollar bill and some loose change.

She stared at the ring as pain zig-zagged through her like a flash of lightning. "This ring meant something to her, something special."

The gold felt warm to her touch as she twisted the circle around and around, trying to see if there was an inscription. The charms on her bracelet tinkled as she moved her wrist.

"Matt," she said as another question rose in her mind. "What about Patti's apartment and the things there? I don't know about furniture, but she must have had clothing and other personal stuff."

"The M.E.'s secretary said we could donate all of it to a local charity. She said they were used to handling things like that. I picked one off a list she gave me. I hope that was okay with you." There was a question at the end.

Kerry nodded.

Matt parked and turned off the engine. "I thought that was too much to ask of strangers—to go through her personal effects and make decisions about them. The secretary assured me all would be taken care of in the proper manner. Whatever that is."

Kerry squeezed his arm. "I couldn't have done all this without you."

He looked into her eyes for a moment, then, unsnapping both their seat belts, he leaned forward and kissed her, briefly but deeply, as if he knew every emotion that raced through her. "Some vacation this has been for you. Maybe someday you'll return and have a better one."

She noticed he didn't include himself in the possible return trip. With a heaviness inside her, she knew, on some deep instinctual level, that she wouldn't return.

"You've already made it as wonderful as possible," she said quietly, sincerely. She even managed a smile.

After they got out and made sure they'd left nothing in the rental car, they went inside. The hotel lobby was the same. The black, gold and burgundy carpet was on the floor, the furniture and plants were still in place, the staff bustled about. Kerry felt so different it seemed the world should reflect that change.

She nodded to Luc Carter, who smiled at them from behind his desk.

Matt went to her suite and deposited the urn before heading for his own quarters to change his clothes. Kerry wanted to freshen up, too, then…

She wasn't sure what came next. Matt was different from any man she'd ever met, more caring, more insightful.

And a wonderful lover.

Sitting down, she hugged her arms across her middle and worried about being too deeply involved in what was, after all, a temporary affair. It was easy for her sister to tell her to enjoy herself, but it was another to become emotionally attached to Matt.

It wasn't her way to fall headlong for someone, but her emotions were confusing. Was the whole situation being blown out of proportion because of Patti's death?

Probably.

Maybe she should stick to her plan to go home Sunday, back where life was normal and she could think clearly.

But she would miss him…

A knock on the connecting door startled her. She unlocked the door and found Matt standing on the other side.

"Okay with you to leave this door open?" he asked.

She nodded, feeling as solemn as an owl.

"Kerry," he said with a laugh, as if reading her sudden uncertainty, and swept her into his arms. "It'll be okay," he whispered, and proceeded to kiss her until she flamed with renewed hunger.

"I thought I wouldn't want this so soon, I mean, after this morning at the inn and during the night—"

She stopped as a hot tide of blood rushed to all parts of her. Ohh, she mentally groaned. She sounded like her great-aunt Martha, the one she and Sharon had labeled "prissy" a long time ago.

She felt the laughter echo in his chest.

He let her down slowly, reluctantly. "Okay, how does coffee, beignets and a planning session sound?"

Her eyes lit up. "I'll forever love beignets."

"Me, too," he agreed, ushering her out to a table in the courtyard.

"Shall we check out the float and its workers this afternoon?" he asked, once they'd been served.

Powdered sugar sifted down Kerry's chin and onto her napkin as she tried to nod while taking a big bite of the delicious doughnut-like confection. They still had the problem of Patti's ashes. She could feel the sadness returning.

"Don't be sad," Matt said, picking up on her change of mood. "I have a feeling Patti wouldn't want you to feel bad or regret what's happened."

Kerry thought of Jason and the love she sensed Patti had for him. "I think, Matt, that we should let Jason Pichante know about the ring. It's a true love's knot, so maybe he gave it to her. He may want it back."

He stirred his coffee and gazed into the distance. "I think you're right. We'll go this afternoon. Around two?"

"Yes."

"After lunch," he said in all innocence, "we'll probably need to rest for an hour or so."

She couldn't stop the snort of laughter. Sugar fluffed out in a white cloud on her black slacks and Matt chuckled. Several people, she saw, glanced at them with smiles on their faces.

She was reminded of a line. *All the world loves a lover?*

Were they...could they possibly be falling in love, really in love?

The answer was easy. She could.

But what about Matt?

PEOPLE SWARMED around the float, diagrams and tools in hand, laughing, chatting and arguing as the work proceeded at a steady pace. For some really weird reason, the float reminded Kerry of the Trojan horse, constructed to look like a gift but designed for deception.

Ashley spotted them as they paused at the open warehouse door. She came over. "You enjoyed yourselves so much the first time, you couldn't stay away, huh?" she teased. "Come on in."

"Oh, you've gotten the garden layout nearly finished," Kerry said, pleased that the structure was actually taking shape. "Do you want to work on the supports again?" she asked Matt.

"May as well."

He smiled in his agreeable manner, and Kerry wanted to give him a bear hug. Which she'd already done during their afternoon nap. Tingles radiated to every point of her body as she thought of their lovemaking.

"Great." Ashley, who was the supervisor of their section when Jason wasn't around, gave them gloves, cable ties and, for Matt, a pair of pliers. "Get to it," she ordered in a friendly manner after showing them where to work.

An hour later, it was time for a break. They selected drinks and cookies from the refreshment cart and settled on the floor, their backs to the wall.

"Is Jason coming in today?" Kerry asked.

Ashley hesitated. "I don't know. He's normally here every afternoon after two, but lately…"

"He hasn't been as reliable?" Matt suggested.

Ashley stared into the distance, a frown on her brow. "There's trouble brewing in that family," she said at last in a low tone. "Jason is very unhappy."

Kerry, noting the worry in the other woman's eyes, wondered if Ashley was interested in the Pichante scion. Was she a suitable match for Jason, one his family would approve and encourage?

A terrible pain lodged in the center of Kerry's being. She glanced at Matt's handsome, attentive face. Was *she,* a small-town hygienist, suitable for someone like him, a sophisticated wine expert?

But Matt was at ease everywhere he went, she thought. He was just as comfortable and charming among the warehouse workers as he'd been with the members of that exclusive country club.

Had that only been a few nights ago?

She counted back. Yes, the dinner, wine-tasting and dance had been on Monday night. Today was Thursday. They'd met on Saturday night. Not even a full week and they were as involved as if they'd been together for months...years...eternity.

Old money, he'd said of his family. While he didn't seem particularly close to them, it was still a different world from the one she inhabited.

And why was she thinking about something that was totally irrelevant to her life? After this week, each of them would be a fond memory for the other, two strangers who'd met under rather eerie circumstances and whose lives had intertwined for a few days.

She sighed. There were other things to be taken care of at present. "Ashley," she began, "Matt and I want to perform a healing ceremony for Patti—"

Ashley interrupted her. "One of the workers said you were at a healing ceremony with the old voodoo queen last Sunday. She said the queen said you should do a cleansing ceremony."

Kerry wondered if the worker was as the young voodoo queen who'd led them back to the taxi. "We were told a cremation would take care of the cleansing. That's done. Now we want to scatter the ashes where Patti's spirit will find rest. Do you have any ideas about that?"

For a second, Ashley looked as if she might burst into tears, then she shook her head. "Did you try to find the plantation, the one I told you about?"

"Patti never lived at Cordon Rouge," Matt spoke up. "It was a ruin, long reverted to swamp, before she was born."

"Then I don't know." Her face brightened. "Here comes Jason. Maybe he can tell you." She rose. "Jason! Over here."

Kerry's eyes met Matt's. He frowned, then shrugged slightly as if accepting the inevitable.

"Jason," Ashley said when he came over to them, "Kerry and Matt have some questions about Patti, about what to do with her ashes. I thought you might have some ideas." She glanced at her watch. "I've got to get back to work."

With that, she walked off, leaving Kerry, Matt and Jason eyeing each other in dead silence.

"Let's go outside," he said abruptly and headed for the door as if the fires of hell nipped at his heels.

Matt took Kerry's arm and helped her up, then they followed Jason outside the warehouse and down the street to a small park. Jason stopped by a bench under the shade of an oak tree draped with moss. The wind from the river caused the strands of moss to swish back and forth.

An image of Patti and her long, beautiful tresses came to Kerry.

"What do you want?" Jason said, ungracious to the point of rudeness.

Matt nodded at Kerry.

She took a slow, deep breath, then asked, "Were you with Patti when she died?"

Jason's darkly handsome face looked as if it had been carved from stone at the question, but he didn't answer.

"Did you buy her the love potion?" Kerry continued. Anger rose in her at his stark silence. It seemed a denial of Patti and the love she'd had for him. "Did you abandon her when she became ill?"

Jason's face turned white. The red spots formed on his cheeks as they had once before when they had asked him about Patti. He opened his mouth, closed it. Finally he turned to the tree, put his forearm on it and pressed his face into the crook of his elbow.

She felt his sorrow, his regret, his shame, and began to tremble herself. Matt stepped closer to put a supportive hand at the small of her back, and she leaned into him, needing his strength.

After a moment, when Kerry wondered if they should leave, Jason began to speak. His voice was so hoarse, it was difficult to hear him over the traffic noises.

"I was with her," he said. "I didn't…I didn't abandon her. She said she felt ill and was going to the restroom, but then I saw her go into one of the patios along the courtyard. I went over there to rescue her before someone thought she was a thief or something."

"And then?" Kerry asked.

"She wasn't there. The door was open and a lamp was on. The bed had been turned down and…and Patti was on it. I tried to tell her we had to leave, but she held my hand and wouldn't let go. I realized she was having trouble breathing."

Kerry put her arm around Matt and held on as wave after wave of dizziness washed over her. She recalled the patient who had clawed at her throat when she couldn't breathe.

"I tried CPR," Jason said, lifting his head and staring at them, his eyes dark and desperate. "I tried, but she shook her head and…and touched my face… then she simply closed her eyes…as if she'd gone to sleep."

The wind through the oak made rustling sounds, as if nature were mourning with them.

"What happened after that?" Matt demanded.

"I panicked. I thought of how it would look—me in a hotel room with Patti. The scandal. My father would be furious. He wanted to announce my engagement to someone else during our annual Mardi Gras party."

"Dear God," Kerry whispered, her heart aching for Patti and, oddly, for Jason.

"Patti was gone, there was nothing else I could do for her, so I left." His voice was flat and harsh and unforgiving.

Of himself, Kerry realized.

Matt urged her to the bench and sat beside her, his arm around her.

Her eyes met Jason's.

"There's nothing you can say, nothing you can call me that I haven't said or called myself," he said bitterly.

"Did you love her?" she asked softly.

A muscle jerked in his jaw. "Yes." Jason's expressive mouth curled in disgust. "But not enough to defy my father for her. Or to risk scandal. As if it mattered what anyone else thought."

On that bitter note, he turned toward the warehouse. "If there's nothing else…"

"There is," Kerry said. She removed the gold ring from her purse. "The medical examiner's office gave us the things she had with her. This ring was the only valuable item. Did you give it to her?"

He stared at the ring lying on her palm. "Yes. It's supposed to represent true love. I guess mine wasn't very reliable, was it?"

Kerry held it out toward him. "It looks expensive. You probably want it back."

"*Mon Dieu*," he muttered. He shook his head violently. "Never. I can't...I can't touch it."

The silence stretched between them again.

"What should I do with it?" she asked.

"I don't know. I don't care. Throw it in the river."

With that, he stalked off, heading back to the warehouse and the work that must keep him from thinking about Patti and how he'd failed her and betrayed their love.

From the river, they heard the sound of a calliope playing a lively air. It seemed surreal.

"Are you okay?" Matt asked after a while.

She nodded and gave him a wan smile to show him that she really was. "It's just that I feel so sorry for him. Isn't that odd? I mean, he doesn't deserve it..."

"Perhaps he does," Matt told her. "He lost something he may never regain—respect for himself."

MATT WAS VERY GENTLE with Kerry that afternoon. They walked along the river for almost two hours. At one point she removed the ring from her purse and contemplated it, then the river. He knew she was thinking of tossing it into the water and letting the river spirit claim it.

With a sigh, she returned it to her purse.

He wasn't indifferent to Patti and her fate or to Jason and his guilt and misery, but he knew he didn't feel the impact as deeply as Kerry did. She was a sympathetic person and family-oriented.

While he'd learned from his former fiancée not to take people at face value, he was sure Kerry was sincere in the pity she felt for the young couple. He stayed close but gave her the emotional space she needed to regain her spirits.

At dusk, they returned to the hotel. Kerry looked weary, but he thought she'd found peace within herself.

After a quiet dinner in the hotel dining room, they returned to her suite and sat on the enclosed patio, sipping a sweet merlot he'd found on the wine menu.

"You were wonderful today, Matt," she said after almost an hour of silence.

"Hardly."

"Yes. You somehow knew I needed to walk and not talk, not even to think, really. You must have been bored, but it was comforting to have you with me."

"Being with you doesn't bore me," he assured her.

She gazed at him for a long moment. "I think...I think I may go home on Sunday as originally planned."

Somehow he wasn't surprised by her announcement, but it did send a funny, painful pang right through him. That didn't surprise him, either. "Let's not make any hasty decisions," he suggested carefully. "Things may look brighter tomorrow."

Her smile was sweet but unconvinced. "My grand-mother often says the same thing."

"I hope you believe everything your grandmother tells you," he said on a lighter note.

She nodded. "Absolutely."

His heart leaped to see she'd regained some of her buoyancy.

"I think I'll get ready for bed, maybe catch the news on TV and see if the rest of the world is still out there," she said.

"Good idea."

She went inside her room and closed the door. He sat there for a while as the night enfolded him com-pletely. Finally he went through his patio to his room. The adjoining door was closed. Okay, she needed some time alone. He could understand that.

But he didn't have to like it, he admitted wryly as he slipped into pajama bottoms and settled on a chair to watch the evening news. The world seemed pretty much the same as it had been five days ago when he'd arrived in New Orleans.

The difference, he concluded, was in himself. He gazed at the closed door.

When it opened, he thought at first it was his imag-ination.

Kerry, dressed in her modest pajamas and wearing her red robe, poked her head around the frame. "My bed or yours?" she asked, her gaze luminous, her man-ner warm, inviting, trusting.

He went to her and swept her effortlessly into his arms. "Let's try them both and see which is the most comfortable."

Her soft laughter smoothed all the bumps of the afternoon and stilled the doubts in him. For a while he'd worried that she might not want to have anything to do with him, that she might think he was interested only in the physical relationship between them...that he was as shallow in his feelings as Jason had been with Patti.

Later, after many sweet kisses and caresses, they shared a last glass of the merlot. He gazed into her eyes, now dreamy with repletion, the haunted look dimmed, although not completely gone.

In the lamplight, her eyes seemed darker than they really were. The irises were wide and the brown flecks overshadowed the lighter shades of green that seemed to dominate in the sunlight.

She was a woman of contrasts—candid but with her own feminine mysteries, kind but with a firm code of loyalty that she expected others to share. He thought Jason had failed in that department and found that he shared her pity for the younger man.

To have a great love and throw it away was a terrible waste of a priceless gift. His heart gave that funny lurch he'd experienced of late—since he'd met Kerry, he acknowledged, feeling a rush of warmth throughout his being.

"Kerry," he murmured when she took a final sip of

the wine, then snuggled close as if intent on going to sleep.

She stifled a yawn. "Yes?"

"Don't go home this weekend. I don't think I can give you up. Not yet," he added to forestall the refusal he was sure he detected in her eyes.

Maybe not ever? some curious part of him inquired.

"I'll think about it," she promised and closed her eyes as if determined not to speak further about it.

CHAPTER ELEVEN

KERRY STUDIED the urn while she sipped the hot coffee Matt had served her in bed. He'd ordered breakfast sent to her suite and they'd eaten in there. After the meal, he'd left for an appointment with a reporter who wrote an entertainment column for the local paper. The guy wanted to interview Matt about his impressions of New Orleans.

From this discussion, she'd learned one more bit of distressing news—Matt had written several bestselling books and was *really* well known in wine and entertainment circles.

Sitting on the bed with pillows piled behind her back, she scanned the reporter's current column. The headline read: Wine Expert Gives His Seal of Approval. That referred to the tasting at the country club the other night. The journalist promised a full feature in Sunday's paper on Matt's activities while in the city.

Not all his activities, she thought. The article wouldn't mention his strange meeting with her Saturday night and the strange journey they'd been on ever since.

She sighed, then quickly checked the obituary pages, but there was nothing. Kerry called the paper and spoke to the person in charge of that section. She asked if they'd received any information on Patti Ruoui.

"Yes," the woman said, "we received the information from the police report and ran the item Wednesday. I have another call. Is there anything else?"

"No. Thanks very much."

Kerry hung up and perused the urn once more. Wednesday. That was the day she and Matt went to Cajun country to find a resting place for Patti. She wondered if Patti's aunt and uncle had read their niece's obituary.

She had to go back out there, she realized. She had to find the place of Patti's dreams, not her happiness.

Somehow knowing this was the last step in the quest, Kerry called her sister. She asked about the children first.

"The little dears are pretty much cleared up," Sharon reported. "The two oldest are back in school and Mom took the four-year-old for the day so I could go to lunch with my book club pals. Not that I had a chance to read our latest selection," she added.

"I discovered something about Matt today," Kerry said.

Her sister chortled. "Does he have a mole in an interesting place?" she teased. "Is he a great lover?"

Kerry rolled her eyes but answered honestly. "I don't recall any moles, but yes to the last question."

"Oh, Kerry, you *are* having an adventure," Sharon said in mock envy. "All we're having is snowstorms."

"Getting back to the subject," Kerry said pointedly, "Matt not only comes from old money, but apparently has made a bundle on his own. In addition to a regular column in a glitzy magazine, he's written some books, that did very well."

"Oh my gosh!" Sharon squealed in her ear. "Matt Anderson. Of course. My book club read *The Good Life* two years ago. It was on all the nonfiction best-seller lists for months. His bio said he'd written two others before that, one about selecting wines for a private cellar. I don't recall what the other was about. Wow, classy circles you're running in."

Kerry agreed, then changed the subject to Patti and the need to find a resting place for her.

"Did you find any more info on the Ruoui family?" she asked.

"Some," Sharon said. "Let me get the printout. I have the name of the plantation where the aunt and uncle live. Apparently it's across the bayou from the original Ruoui home place."

"Hold on. I'll write that down."

"You and Matt are really spending a lot of time to-gether," Sharon remarked after relating all she had found in newspaper articles on Cordon Rouge and the family that had once inhabited it. "Do you think you'll keep in touch after you come home?"

"Why would we?" Kerry asked. "We live in different worlds. I'm sure he would die of boredom in Minnesota." She managed a light laugh, as if it didn't really matter.

"Well, maybe you'll exchange Christmas cards or hey, he might invite you to New York for a long weekend. You could go to the theater and wine tastings. Maybe you'll meet his snooty family."

"Matt isn't snooty," Kerry quickly jumped in to defend him in case her sister had gotten the wrong impression.

"Obviously," Sharon agreed. "He sounds like one of the good guys to me. I don't think you should let go of him so easily."

"We don't have anything in common."

There, she'd stated the awful truth of the situation. What did she have in common with a New York wine expert and writer who came from "old money"?

Not much. Other than the most sizzling physical relationship she'd ever experienced. But their relationship was more than just sex. He'd offered her emotional support. Matt hadn't drawn away as a lot of men would have when she'd wept or been sad or indignant about the people in Patti's life.

"Well, time to get ready for the luncheon," Sharon said. "See you—are you still coming home on Sunday?"

"Yes, I think that would be best."

"Hmm," her sister said. "Think about what you're doing. Take care."

"Right," Kerry said. She clicked off the cell phone. "I think," she murmured, "that I've fallen in love."

Was that possible? In less than a week?

She realized it was going to hurt to leave Matt, much more than it had when she'd returned her fiancé's ring and wished him and his new love a long and happy life. Much, much more.

BY THE TIME Matt returned, Kerry was sure of her decisions, all of them. She would mention them at lunch.

After talking to her sister, she'd also called the airlines. She could still take her scheduled flight out on Sunday or one at the same time the following Wednesday. There was plenty of space on either.

She questioned the wisdom of prolonging her stay. Each added day would only make it that much more difficult to leave this wonderful man.

Sighing, she put her personal problems on hold. She had a mission to complete. If her instincts were correct about Patti's spiritual home, that mission should be fulfilled by tomorrow. Then she could leave on Sunday as planned.

Observing Matt remove his suit jacket and tie, toss them on a chair, roll up his shirt sleeves, then come to her, she felt as if her heart were being squeezed into a knot as intricate as the one on Patti's ring.

"I'm glad that's over. I prefer being the interviewer, not the interviewee," he said, then tilted her face to his for a quick kiss.

His laugh flowed over her, into her, lodging in the very recesses of her heart. She would always remember him and their time in, for her, the most magical city in the world.

She realized she was already feeling nostalgic about every moment. There weren't many left to remember.

"Okay, what're our plans for the day?" he asked, eyeing her outfit.

Shortly before he was due back, she'd dressed in a long, full skirt of gold sunflowers on a black background with a white shell under a reverse print shirt of the same sunflower pattern. Her sister had talked her into getting it. At the appreciative look in his eyes, she was glad she had.

Her hair had lightened from the hours she'd spent in the sun that week and had formed natural highlights around her face. She'd even gotten a slight tan.

Glancing in the mirror as Matt pulled her from the chair, she realized she had never looked better. And that she and Matt made a very good-looking couple.

MATT COULDN'T take his eyes off Kerry at lunch. They'd decided to try a different restaurant in the Quarter for lunch, but something had changed between them, and he didn't know what. Kerry was back to her talkative self, but she avoided his eyes.

Yeah, that's what was different. It was as if she was trying to hide something from him. The idea bothered him more than it should have.

"Sightseeing," she suggested during lunch. "Since you're finished with appointments for the rest of the day, I thought we might stroll through the French Market. I've walked down Bourbon Street, but I haven't been to Basin. Have you?"

"Not yet. Okay, we've got a plan for the afternoon. I thought we could dine in Chez Remy this evening, then, according to the concierge, there'll be dancing at nine. I want to dance with you again."

"Yes," she said, her eyes gleaming, the darker shades around the irises reminding him of the coral he'd explored beneath the sea's surface. "I love to dance, especially with someone as good as you."

"Careful, I'll get a swelled head."

He laughed when she did, and all seemed normal between them. "Ready?" he asked. "I have something I want to get."

"What?" She put a hand over her mouth and looked chagrined. "I'm sorry, Matt. I'm treating you like a member of my family. We're always minding each other's business."

"From what you've said, no one gets upset."

"Well, sometimes we tell the other person to butt out. I think I'm going to have to tell my sister to do that—"

When she stopped abruptly, Matt shot her a questioning glance. When Kerry didn't say more, he asked, "Is she giving you advice about this vacation?"

"Sort of."

That's all he could get her to admit after they paid the bill and headed up the street. They checked out the French Market, where Matt got a lesson in haggling as, amused and astounded, he listened to Kerry talk a street vendor down to half price, then less as she offered a flat fee for the purses and leather wallets she purchased for various members of her family.

When the man acted as if he was going to refuse, she took Matt's arm and said, "Let's go."

"Hold on," the vendor told her. "You're robbing my kid's college fund, but I'll take it." However, after the deal was concluded, the man smiled broadly and shook Kerry's hand. "It's been a pleasure doing business with you."

Her laughter brought smiles to everyone who heard it. "The pleasure was mine," she told the vendor.

Walking on down the street, Matt said, "How much would you charge to handle my business affairs from now on?"

Her grin was deliberately calculating. "I'll cut you a special deal."

"Ha. You'll probably charge me double."

On that note, they left the area and headed away from the river. A couple of blocks before they reached Basin Street, he guided her into a right turn. "Just a quick detour."

He found the jewelry store recommended by the hotel's concierge. Inside they were waited on at once.

"Luc Carter at the Hotel Marchand said you had a good selection of spirit charms in your store."

"Yes," the clerk assured them. "These three cases. Are you looking for sterling silver or something in gold?"

Matt glanced at the charm bracelet Kerry wore. "Silver to match the lady's bracelet," he said.

Kerry's eyes opened wide. "Matt, you're not buying a charm for me," she protested.

"Who else would I get one for? You need the Spirit of Wisdom, remember?"

"Yes, but you don't have to—"

"Ah, that would be the snake," the man said. He removed two trays from the display case.

"You shouldn't—"

Matt laid a finger over her delectable lips. "Be a gracious receiver," he said firmly. "I want you to have it to remember our time here."

"As if I could ever forget." She smiled at the clerk. "I've had the most fascinating week in your lovely city."

The man was obviously pleased.

Kerry, Matt realized, had the ability to make people feel good about themselves. That was certainly the way he felt around her. He gestured toward the jewelry trays. "Which do you like?"

After studying the charms, she chose a very simple design, one that was probably the least expensive of all the items. Matt spotted another on the second tray that he liked.

"How about this one?" he suggested. "It looks like the python—you know, the one you had your picture taken with."

It also had emeralds for the eyes, and the gems reminded him of hers. When they made love, the shade seemed to change from peridot to dark emerald.

The heat that swept through him told him to keep his mind on the present moment, but it was damn hard to do.

"That must have been Madame Jolie," the salesman said, his eyes filled with admiration as he looked at Kerry.

Matt refrained from flatly telling the guy she wasn't available. That wasn't his call, he reminded himself ruthlessly. Did he want it to be? Did he want a permanent bond between them?

"Yes, it was." Kerry beamed at the man, then leaned over the tray and studied the charm Matt had suggested. "Are those emeralds?" she asked.

"They are," the clerk assured her. "Small but genuine. And a very good quality."

The concierge had said the store was known for its integrity and care in selecting jewels, which was why Matt had brought Kerry here.

He leaned close to her. "They remind me of your eyes," he murmured. "We'll take it," he told the man behind the counter.

"How much is it?" Kerry demanded, giving him a stern glance.

To his amazement, she got a ten percent discount

on the charm. She glanced at him with great satisfaction, and he couldn't help but return her grin.

"We also need a Spirit of Healing," he said.

"Oh, yes, we have thunder charms, too." The clerk quickly pulled out a tray depicting a cloud with a zigzag of lightning running through it to symbolize thunder.

Matt selected the one he wanted, then stood back while Kerry got him a better price. When all was finished, he asked the clerk to attach them to her bracelet rather than boxing them.

When they left the store, Kerry was quiet. After she'd inspected the charms for the third time, he asked if she liked them.

"Oh, yes. I can't thank you enough for getting them for me."

"Then what's the problem?" He had another thought. "I can afford them, Kerry," he added quietly.

"No, it isn't that, but…I can't think of anything to give you."

He burst into laughter.

She studied him suspiciously while waiting for him to regain control.

"Darling, the last two days have been the best gift I've ever had." He cupped her face in his hands. "I mean that." Then he kissed her. Deeply. And much too briefly.

"Okay, I believe you. I think."

He had to laugh again as her lips pursed in doubt. It took all his control not to kiss her again.

Holding hands, they strolled along the street made

famous by the blues song written in its honor. The shadows were long by the time they returned to the hotel. After leaving her package in her suite, they returned to the courtyard and their favorite table for an afternoon drink.

"Funny," he said, "how quickly people establish a pattern. We always sit at this table. That older couple over there always sit under that tree near the pool."

She turned to look at the other pair, who were probably in their seventies. "I wonder if this is their first time here, or if they've returned every year for, say, fifty years, on their wedding anniversary."

"Now that's a thought," he murmured. "How many marriages last that long?"

"Well, both sets of my grandparents and their parents, too. All except one of my great-grandfathers who died of a heart attack when he was sixty. My mom and dad will probably make it."

He studied her for a moment.

"What?" she asked.

"Why hasn't some smart guy grabbed you up long before this?" He took her left hand in his and rubbed up and down her ring finger. "You haven't mentioned divorce, so I assume you haven't been married."

"No, but I was engaged." She gave a funny little laugh. "For four years."

"That's a long time. When did you break it off?"

"Six months ago. He's the one who wanted out. He

met an old flame and it was love at second sight, I guess you might say. It was at our class reunion."

Matt didn't like the idea of her being hurt. "Did you live together during that time?"

She shook her head. "We each kept our own place. He had a condo. I have a very small house, inherited from that great-uncle I told you about."

"The one with the drinking problem?"

"Yes. I've loved renovating the cottage. It sits on five acres of land and has a tiny lake teeming with fish. I think he gave it to me because I loved fishing with him and my dad when we visited."

"I see. About your fiancé. I'm sorry you were hurt."

She took his hand between both of hers and pressed it to her cheek. Her eyes sparkled in the last rays of the sun as she told him, "If he felt a tenth of what I feel when we…that is, when…"

"When we make love?" Matt supplied.

"Yes. If it's like that for him with his new fiancée, then he did the right thing. I've never felt anything so intense and exciting. I didn't know it was possible to experience that much sensation."

A part of him that had tensed up when she'd mentioned the ex-fiancé relaxed. "Yeah, I know what you mean."

She released his hand and used the straw to stir her drink, one of those rum-and-fruit concoctions that were fun to try while on vacation. "Being with you has made me realize what I was missing. The old relationship was comfortable. There was mutual respect and common interests, but I don't think…I don't think it was love."

"I see."

"I've confessed all," she said in a low, amused tone. "Now it's your turn. Have you ever been seriously involved with anyone?"

"I was engaged briefly, mmm, about six years ago. I discovered she wanted to be part of my family and their social circle more than she wanted to establish one of our own. Now she's married to someone who keeps up the social pace she wanted."

"Were you hurt?"

"At first," he admitted. "Now when we occasionally run into each other—we have mutual friends—we speak, discuss the weather and go our separate ways."

"Good," she said as if affirming he'd made a wise decision.

He smiled and ordered another drink for each of them.

They sat there in a comfortable silence while evening descended and the courtyard gradually filled with returning guests, weary after a busy day of sightseeing. He saw her touch the charms on her bracelet and the way she smiled as she fingered the snake and the thundercloud.

He was glad he'd bought them. The charms would be a token of their time together and a reminder that once she and a fellow traveler had shared an adventure.

CHAPTER TWELVE

"IT SEEMS ODD to be on this road again," Kerry said as Matt slowed the rental car to the speed limit when they arrived in St. Martinville.

Her eyes were drawn to the statue of Evangeline, then to the inn where she and Matt had spent the night on their own private journey to becoming lovers.

Every nerve in her body tingled at the thought. She couldn't keep from snatching little glances at him while he concentrated on driving. He was so handsome and so *good*—and not just in bed. He was a good person, a phrase her parents used to bestow their highest praise on someone.

"It's déjà vu all over again, as Yogi Berra reputedly said," Matt commented, his smile warm.

"This time we've got to finish what we came for."

"You're still going home tomorrow?"

"I think so." *Unless you can give me a very good reason for staying.* But she didn't say that.

He nodded, his smile never faltering. That was another thing she liked about him—he respected her decisions. He didn't want her to go, he'd stated his case, but the final move was up to her.

So why not stay an extra three days? Or reschedule her appointments and take another week?

Because it would hurt that much more when she did have to leave. Because she might cry and cling to him, and she just wouldn't let herself do that. It seemed better to stick with the original plan.

Sighing, she forced the pesky questions at bay and considered the task ahead. She would stop and speak to Atta about their plan for the ashes, but something inside her said it was the right one.

"Why the sigh?" Matt asked with a quick glance at her.

"I feel certain this is the right thing to do, but then there's this little unsure voice inside me that questions everything."

"That's natural. Who can be one hundred percent sure when it comes to someone elses's wishes?" He paused. "Except in our case," he added softly, a challenge in his deep voice.

"You think we should stay the extra days."

"Absolutely."

She laughed when he gave her a scolding frown. He was too attractive to really look menacing.

"Laugh, woman, but you're breaking my heart."

"Part of me wants to stay…the part that wants to be with you, but another part is ready to leave."

Matt nodded. "It's been a difficult week. Meeting

Patti, then becoming involved in her life, which was tragic in so many ways. It's been emotionally draining on you."

Kerry was silent for a moment. "Thank you for understanding that, Matt. It's one of the things that makes it so hard to think about leaving New Orleans. And you."

"It doesn't have to mean goodbye for us."

"Sharon thought we might visit. She thinks going to New York for a long weekend for the theater and wine tasting sounds great. Of course she's been stuck at home in a snowstorm with three sick kids for most of the week."

"New York doesn't sound interesting to you?"

"Yes, of course it does."

"But?"

Each moment they were together *now* made the thought of a future parting that much more difficult for her. She didn't want to drag out their relationship until one day they realized they were strangers, still clinging to a shared week of mystery and magic. It was better to end things on a happy note.

"This has been one of the best vacations of my life. It's also been one of the worst." She glanced in the backseat at the wooden urn inscribed with voodoo symbols.

"I can identify with that."

"Our lives crossed in a rather dramatic manner, and we became entangled in events not of our making."

"True," he agreed.

"But this isn't our real lives. Mine is in a small town in the Midwest. Yours is in the busy city of New York. After this week, we'll return to those worlds."

"And our paths will never cross again," he concluded.

That sent such a shaft of emotion through her, she couldn't breathe for a second. "Yes."

"But Kerry," he murmured with an oblique glance in her direction as he continued along the bayou road toward Atta's house, "we were obviously fated to meet. Maybe our paths were meant to merge."

She blinked in astonishment at this idea. Touching the charm bracelet, she found the three bones. Three lives, three worlds, three divergent paths...or one shining path leading into the future?

"Do you want to stop?" Matt asked when they reached the small, neat house set amid well-tended flower beds.

"Yes. I think we should tell Atta what we're doing."

He pulled into the drive.

"I'll go to the door," Kerry volunteered.

She dashed up the brick walk and knocked on the door. No one answered. The place had an air of emptiness, Matt observed. She knocked again. Still no answer. She returned to the car.

"She doesn't appear to be at home," she said.

"Maybe she's shopping or visiting with family."

"I guess. I didn't get the impression she had much family left, did you?"

"Well, I suppose if you last long enough, you might outlive most of them."

Kerry nodded, climbing into the car. They continued along the weed-choked lane, the twin tracks barely visible among the grass and thistles.

"This was once a carriage road," he said. "Can't you just see the fancy rigs arriving for a ball, the matched sets of horses prancing as they entered the drive, the ladies and gentlemen in their best party clothes."

"The lane would be lined with lanterns," Kerry added, continuing the tale. "A hundred or more candles would brighten the house."

"You would be the belle of the ball," he told her, and he could almost see her in a beautiful gown. Who would be her escort? he wondered.

Not him, came the answer from deep within.

"There," Kerry said. "There, among the trees. I can see a house. The remains of a house," she corrected.

"This may be Cordon Rouge."

He followed the broad curve of the road until they came upon a circular driveway. It led to the ruins of what had obviously been an impressive plantation house.

Chimneys and a crumbling brick foundation were visible amid a mad tangle of vines. Three corners of the house still stood and most of a porch. In places, remains of balconies supported by columns still covered the porch below. Although the roof was long gone, the foundation defined the perimeter of a mansion. It was more than twice as big as the farmhouse where Patti had lived.

"There were porches with balconies on the front and two sides," Matt pointed out. "Probably in the back as well."

Oaks, draped in Spanish moss, curved around the circular carriageway and along a wide path that disappeared behind the building. In fact, brick paths were visible all around the grounds.

Beyond the house ruins, he could see a bayou, its banks lush with reeds and wild rice. Bayou Rouge. He wondered how it had gotten its name. It wasn't red, as rouge implied, but brown, thanks to the release of tannin from decaying plants.

"Even though it's been untended for seventy years, it's easy to imagine what the place once looked like," he said to Kerry. "It must have been impressive."

She nodded. "Let's go around to the back. I don't see a flower garden from here." She pointed to one side. "That appears to have been a shrub garden. Some of the bushes are still there, but everything's way overgrown."

Matt retrieved the urn and gave it to her. Bringing it to her chest, she held it with both hands and started through the weeds.

"Let's use the porch," he suggested.

They went up brick steps that were at least eight feet

wide—"to have room for those hoop skirts," Kerry suggested, giving him a smile for the first time since they'd arrived—and went to the back of the mansion.

He held her arm as they carefully picked out the firm planks and avoided those that were broken. The porch wrapped around all sides, he saw.

"There's the garden," Kerry said.

The area was perhaps a quarter of an acre, surrounded by a low rock wall and located halfway between the house and bayou. Tall, graceful pine trees marked each corner. A sidewalk led from the back steps down through the middle of the enclosure. A jardiniere on a pedestal in the middle of a large basin formed the center of the garden and was the focal point from the house.

"That was once a fountain," Kerry said. "Don't you think so?"

"Yes." Holding Kerry's arm, he led the way along the walk and stopped before the dry basin.

The sunlight caught her eyes as she glanced up at him, then around the enclosure. "This was once a *parterre* or patterned formal garden. You can still see the layout from the brick paths although the flowers and shrubs are gone now. Look, a wild rose has invaded that corner."

Matt glanced where she pointed. Pale pink flowers grew on the wall near one of the pine trees that stood like a sentinel at the garden's corner.

"That would be a good place to sprinkle her ashes, wouldn't it?" he asked, ushering her toward the spot.

Odd, but he felt the need to get Kerry away from the old plantation, which was gradually returning to the marsh. The place felt eerie, as if it would suck the soul out of someone as sensitive as she was.

"Yes," she said. "I think we should scatter them along the four sides of the garden." Her voice was low, subdued, as if she was hesitant to disturb any spirits that lingered in this forlorn place.

Unable to dispel his illogical worry, Matt followed Kerry as she sprinkled the ashes down each fence line.

"To the gentle spirit of the east wind," she said at the end of the path leading to the stone wall in that direction. A rusted wrought-iron bench was discernible through a mound of vines. She opened the urn and sprinkled the ashes in the space between the wall and the brick path.

They returned to the middle of the garden, then walked to the north wall, where the path continued to the house. "To the restless spirit of the north wind," she said and left a trail of ashes. "To the adventurous spirit of the west wind," she intoned at that wall, and finally, "To the wise spirit of the south wind."

He breathed a sigh of relief when the job was done and the urn was empty.

"I suppose we'd better head back," he said.

She nodded, but didn't move. "There's a niche in the pedestal holding the big vase. We can put the urn there."

Returning to the center of the garden, he held her

hand while she stepped over the shell-shaped edge of the basin and set the carved urn into the narrow recess, which seemed as if it had been made for this purpose.

"There were statues in these niches, I think," Kerry said, clasping his hand to climb out. "Someone must have taken them, but you can see where the round bases were attached once upon a time."

Her last words lingered in his mind. *Once upon a time.*

Fairy-tale words. Once upon a time, a child and her parents lived on a magical plantation surrounded by pines and oaks and a bayou where crayfish and dragonflies played all day. Life was perfect.

But of course it hadn't been.

He wondered if he and this petite, caring woman would look back on this week as a time out of their lives, that had drawn them close for a few days before they'd resumed their real lives. Kerry had made it pretty clear that was what she wanted.

"The sidewalk goes to the bayou," she said. "Let's walk out there."

Still holding hands, they made their way around the old fountain, following the walkway to the water. He noted the slant of the shadows on the stream. The sun was still fairly high above the stand of cypress trees west of them, where the bayou curved out of sight. At night, this place would be spooky with the moss swaying from the trees and the wind moaning through the grasses.

He thought of ghosts and vengeful spirits. Although he didn't believe in such things, he wouldn't want to be caught back here in the swampland after dark. The road had been hard enough to follow during daylight hours, and he wanted Kerry safely back in the city long before the sun went down.

"We should leave soon," he reminded her.

She nodded and let go of his hand, her eyes on the darkly flowing ribbon of water as if drawn to it by forces she couldn't resist.

At the end of the sidewalk, he saw posts that indicated a pier had once stood there to welcome visitors by boat. Only a skeleton of broken planks remained. Kerry, he noted, was fingering the bracelet on her left arm, moving from one charm to the next like a nun saying her rosary.

Again he felt uneasy, though he couldn't say why.

"There's a house over there," she said. "A car is going up the driveway."

Matt followed her line of vision across the bayou. The sun glinted off a windshield, then another and another.

"More than one," he said.

"Maybe they're having a party, a grand afternoon tea. Do people still do those?"

A smile touched her lips, now bare of lipstick, but lush and pink nevertheless. Matt suppressed the hunger that was never far from the surface when he was with Kerry.

"I think it's called bridge club these days," Matt teased.

Across the tall grasses that waved in the slight breeze, they could hear voices calling greetings to each other. Again it seemed as if they'd stepped into another era—one of carriages and tea parties and fancy balls.

After the guests went inside the mansion, all was quiet. Kerry turned to him. "Patti's aunt and uncle live there. My sister found the address for me. I saw the name scrolled in wrought iron over a driveway before we made the last turn coming here." She turned back to the grand country house across the bayou. "That's where she lived as an orphan."

He saw Kerry touch the bracelet again. She was so pensive he slipped an arm around her and held her close to him, the protective urge so strong he couldn't deny it. There was something fragile about her, as if she might shatter if touched too roughly.

"Atta said Patti was unhappy there." Kerry nodded toward the house, her hand enclosing the bracelet.

"Yes," he said.

"But I think she was happy here."

As if released from an enchantment, they turned as one and surveyed the old plantation house. Kerry smiled up at him. "This was the right thing to do. I can feel it." She held up her arm so he could see the charm bracelet. "We have done good *Ju-Ju* today. All the roaming spirits are now at rest here."

She opened her hand. He saw the gold ring on her palm. He waited, thinking she might throw it into the water, but she stood there a few seconds, then slipped it back into the pocket of her jeans. The ring was still a problem.

On the return trip, they drove past the cottage, but no one was on the porch, so Matt didn't stop.

Farther along the road, they passed a church and a small cemetery. "Can we stop?" Kerry asked softly.

He did so reluctantly, feeling that she had had enough emotional stress for one day, but he respected her request. He pulled into the neatly maintained driveway and parked under the shade of an oak heavy with moss.

"This may be the parish cemetery where Patti's folks are buried," she said when they got out of the car. She held out her hand to him.

Matt noted that they automatically held hands when they were together. He wondered if Kerry noticed.

"What?" she asked.

He held up their clasped hands. "I'm reminded of my sister. Since she was four years older, she insisted on holding my hand while crossing the street. At five, I rebelled, telling her I could do it by myself. She informed me if I got run over it would be my own stupid fault. Now I find I like holding hands."

Kerry gave him one of her warm glances. "Me, too," she murmured, looking away. "Were you and your sister friends?"

He felt a slight distancing on her part and resisted the urge to hold her tighter. "Yes. When I was in high school and she was in college, I'd call her when I had woman trouble and she'd explain the female psyche to me. Not that I always believed her, but mostly she was right. As we grew up, she became my best friend."

"Sharon and I are close, too." She hesitated. "I'm glad you had your sister. Everyone needs someone to connect to, especially if your parents aren't—I mean—"

"I know what you mean, Kerry," he assured her. "My parents lived their lives as they saw fit. So do I. If I'm ever blessed with a family, I want to be part of my children's lives."

She gave him a glowing look of approval, making him feel as if he was the wisest man in the world.

"Oh, look," she said, pointing to a vault. "Ruoui. That's Patti's family name."

They studied the names in the area and found the graves went back several generations. "Almost two hundred years," he remarked. "That's a long history."

"Yes, and Patti knew where their first ancestor to settle here came from, too. She told me she was related to Josephine Bonaparte. Seeing how far back her ancestors go makes me believe her story."

"I wonder if she was the last of the Ruoui line."

A shadow crossed Kerry's face, darkening her eyes. "I think she must be. She had no siblings and her aunt hasn't any children." She surveyed the richly carved marble and granite vaults. "I can envision Patti here as a child, walking with her parents and listening to her father recount dashing tales about their ancestors. It must have given her a sense of continuity, don't you think?"

He nodded.

"And now that line is broken," she ended somberly.

They continued strolling and reading the names, dates and messages engraved into the stones. At one site, they paused while Matt read the inscription. "His family hopes his journey proves fortuitous, wherever it may lead." Matt grinned. "It doesn't sound as if they have a lot of hope about where he's going to spend eternity."

Kerry pressed a hand over her mouth.

"What?" he demanded, seeing the amusement in her eyes.

"When Sharon and I were kids, we went to our great-aunt's funeral. She was our grandmother's only sister, and she was a stickler for manners and rather mean to us kids. When Nana dropped a handful of dirt on her coffin, Sharon and I recited, 'Ashes to ashes, dust to dust; if the Lord won't have you, then the devil must.' I thought my mom was going to faint from mortification, but everyone else, including my grandmother and the pastor, burst into laughter. I think that saved us from being grounded for life."

The tension went out of his shoulders at seeing her back to her usual buoyant self. "My father," he confided, "would have had a coronary if my sister and I had done anything like that."

They laughed together in perfect understanding. It felt good. From that first odd moment when she'd come over to help him with the unknown woman in his bed, being with Kerry had felt good. He had a feeling if he let her disappear from his life he would miss something important in his future.

After reading a few more inscriptions, they returned to the car and headed for the city. Matt saw Kerry's eyes held only humor and the nostalgia of gentle memories. Contentment filled his own soul.

BACK IN NEW ORLEANS, Kerry kept an eye out for a parking space as Matt cruised the block around the hotel for the second time.

"There's one," she said as a car vacated a spot.

Matt whipped in and parallel parked with no problem.

"You're good," she declared. "I always manage to either run into the curb or have one end of the car sticking out into the street. There must be a secret to it that no one has told me about."

"Most people don't pull up close enough to the car ahead before they start backing up."

"Aha, I knew there was something I'd missed."

Laughing, they linked hands and went into the hotel. A man rose from a chair and came to Kerry.

"I need to talk to you," Jason Pichante told her. He glanced at Matt. "Alone."

"I'll be in the suite," Matt said after she gave him a nod to indicate she was okay to be alone with Jason.

Kerry didn't miss the glance he sent the younger man, as if warning him he'd better not hurt her feelings.

"There are chairs over here," Jason said.

He led the way to an alcove containing a tiny table and two brocaded chairs. From here they could look out on the street where Saturday night revelers had already gathered. By contrast, she noted, the hotel lobby, other than staff and a few people going through to their rooms, was empty.

She studied the younger man, waiting for him to tell her his reason for being there. His handsome face showed the ravages of grief. There were fresh lines across his forehead and darker circles under his eyes. The planes of his cheeks and jaw were still handsome and aristocratic looking, but they seemed leaner, too, more sharply etched.

"Do you want the ring?" she asked quietly.

He tore his gaze from the street scene and stared at her. He shook his head. "Keep it for your daughter. Advise her of the futility of loving a coward."

"Is that how you see yourself?"

"It's what I am." He spoke without any visible emotion. "I wanted to tell you the truth of that night before I go."

"You're leaving New Orleans?"

"Yes. I've told my parents. And my fiancée."

Her heart constricted at the word, and she thought of Patti, who had loved this man.

He took a deep breath. "That night...Twelfth Night... I told Patti about the engagement and the announcement that would be made at my parents' party. She was stunned. I told her it wouldn't make any difference to us."

Kerry couldn't suppress the tiny gasp his words caused. "You wanted her for your mistress after you married someone else?"

"Yeah. Some Twelfth Night gift, wasn't it?" he said with a bitter laugh.

Kerry stared at him without answering.

He continued. "We were sitting in the courtyard here at the hotel. We'd been dancing, and she was laughing as some tourists stared at our outfits. After I told her of the engagement, she said she couldn't see me again. She stood, ready to walk out on me, but I pulled her into my arms and started to dance. I asked her to let me explain.

"I told her the marriage was necessary because the girl's father held credit notes from my father that he was threatening to call. The family would be ruined if...if I didn't comply. Politically, it was a good marriage. Patti understood that."

"Did she agree to be the third party in this arrangement?"

"No. She said if the engagement was announced, she would take that as the end for us."

"Good for her," Kerry murmured.

He stared out the window again as if seeing

another time, another place. "An old woman came through the courtyard selling flowers and herbal concoctions. I bought two bottles of love potion. Giving one to Patti, I challenged her to drink it. I said it would make her mine forever. She told me to be careful, that it might make me forget the politically correct marriage and bind our hearts for all eternity instead."

Kerry nodded. Patti had evidently believed in the power of love and potions and portent, which came as no surprise to Kerry.

"I asked her to give me that one night if that was all we were to have. She didn't answer, but she stayed. About thirty minutes later, she said she felt ill. That's when she went in search of the restroom and ended up in the patio suite by mistake." He glanced at her, then away. "You know the rest."

"You left her for dead because you couldn't face the scandal of being with Patti when you were supposed to be engaged to another woman?"

"It could have jeopardized my family's position."

Kerry exhaled slowly, carefully. The air around her seemed fragile, as if it might shatter if she moved too quickly or spoke too harshly.

"I don't know about your fiancée," she said, "but Patti was one of the loveliest people I've ever met. I'm not talking about her outward beauty, but the warmth and kindness she showed to me, a stranger, on my first day in New Orleans." She recalled Atta's words. "She had a good soul, so why wasn't she good enough for your family?"

"She had no money, no social standing and no political influence."

The words came so readily to his lips that Kerry was sure he was quoting from his father's many lectures on the subject. Gazing into his dark eyes, she felt a return of the pity and nodded.

Jason stood. "I thought I could have it all—love and marriage and approval. Funny thing, but they all came from different people when they should have come from one. I finally realized that only with Patti could I have had it all. By then it was too late."

Kerry walked to the lobby door with him. They stood there as if facing an abyss that divided two worlds.

Behind them was the austere elegance of the hotel. It seemed to represent a time long ago, a time of grandeur, like the life Patti's family had lived at Cordon Rouge.

In front of them was the busy life on the street, the modern world, a little commercial and crass, but also lively and rich with possibility.

Jason had a choice—step back into his family's world and lose himself...or step forward into the bustling street and find a new life.

"I wish you well on your journey," she told him. "Wherever it may lead."

He surprised her by kissing both her cheeks. "Thank you for caring about Patti. I think you were the only person in her life who didn't fail her." A muscle tightened in his jaw.

"I was only in her life for one day," she reminded him.

He drew a deep breath as he gazed out the door. "I want to ask you something else. Where…"

After a minute of silence, Kerry intuitively grasped the question he couldn't finish. "Matt and I scattered her ashes at Cordon Rouge, in the formal garden there."

He nodded and left her, striding quickly along the street. She watched until he became lost in the crowd.

"Above all, I wish you peace," she whispered. She glanced at the tiny thundercloud charm she was holding. "And healing for your soul."

Then she quickly crossed the lobby and courtyard, heading for the one person she needed beyond all others at this moment.

CHAPTER THIRTEEN

KERRY GLANCED AROUND the room. "That's every-thing," she said. She snapped the locks on the large piece of luggage, which would be checked at the air-lines, and scanned the smaller case with her toiletries.

The bathroom and bedroom were empty of her things and had resumed a rather impersonal air. The concierge had shipped her gift basket home for her, so that was taken care of. She'd wanted it for sentimental purposes—a reminder of the champagne she'd sipped while relaxing in the tub, candles all around her, hearing a noise from next door, meeting Matt during the witching hours of that strange night...Twelfth Night.

She swallowed hard as longing threatened to over-come her. That would never do, not on her last day. She studied Matt, who sat in an easy chair, his attention on the screen of a laptop computer while he worked on his article about New Orleans.

He'd volunteered to drive her to the airport that af-ternoon after a late lunch. They had also had a late breakfast after a very personal leave-taking. They'd eaten at their favorite table in the courtyard.

She was going to miss those lovely, sunny mornings sitting outside, her heart purring like a happy kitten.

"Done?" he asked, his heavenly blue eyes looking up at her.

She nodded, unable to speak for a second.

"You can still change your mind," he said as if the emotion that rose in her was visible to him.

"Charlotte gave me a rain check on another week here," she told him, taking the chair on the other side of the table and sipping the cool coffee in her cup. "Who knows? Maybe I'll come back next year and take in the Mardi Gras parade and parties."

"That's a thought," he agreed, his manner relaxed. "Maybe I will, too."

Her heart leaped at the possibility of being back in New Orleans with him. "So, are you staying the rest of this week?"

"Yes. My editor called and asked if I would check out a couple of new restaurants a friend mentioned to her before I leave. I'm taking you to one of them for lunch before we head for the airport."

"Lucky you. I'm going to miss the warm weather. Sharon said it's below freezing back home."

He chuckled, clicked off the laptop and closed it. "We'd better go."

As they made their way to the rental car, Matt pulled the large suitcase with the smaller case resting on top. She carried a sturdy shopping bag with the gifts for her family members tucked inside.

The charms on her bracelet tinkled against each other like tiny wind chimes. She inhaled deeply, breathing in the scent of the river and salt marshes and the gulf beyond as the breeze caressed her face.

Matt stowed her bags in the trunk, held the car door for her and saw that she was safely inside before getting in and driving down the street, which wasn't very busy.

"I hope things pick up at the hotel," she said, glancing back once at the charming building. "This has been a difficult week for them."

"The concierge said things were getting back to normal, but it's his job to convince guests the hotel is in good shape," Matt said in his deep, pleasant voice. "The Marchand family has certainly had its share of troubles of late."

"And before, too," Kerry told him. "There was Remy's accident and Hurricane Katrina. Also, Charlotte said her mother had had a heart attack a few months ago. She's been very worried about her."

"You and Charlotte got to be friends," he commented.

"Well, not really, but we did have coffee together a couple of times during the week. I liked her. And her mother, too. You remember Anne?"

"Yes. A nice lady. Here we are." He swung the car into a small parking lot in an area of the city that had been rebuilt since the hurricane.

The restaurant had a bold color scheme and deliberately brash attitude, a new, funky place for the young-at-heart, Matt told her.

During the meal, which was based around a tasting menu, there were long lapses in their conversation. Kerry couldn't concentrate. Her emotions were too close to the surface to risk talking. When they at last departed for the airport, she was trapped between relief and despair.

"Well," she said brightly when her luggage was checked and she clutched only the gift bag and her purse. "It's been fun." She gave a little laugh.

"It's been wonderful," he corrected, guiding her to a corner away from the crowd. "Do you have any objections to my calling you at home?"

"No. Of course not. I'd love to hear from you." She gave him her most sincere look while her insides coiled into a tight ball.

"What about visiting? Is that out?"

Startled, she asked, "Would you want to visit White Bear Lake?"

He laughed and shook his head as if highly amused by the question. "I'd like to visit wherever you are."

"Oh. That would be…"

Heaven.

Hell.

Pick one.

"…nice," she finished.

His laughter rolled over her, through her, filling her with impossible yearnings.

She touched his cheek. "I couldn't have made this

journey without you," she said softly. "Never in my wildest imagination could I have come up with a fellow adventurer who was so right for the situation."

"It was fated," he told her without a trace of irony or sardonic wit. He took her hand, touched each charm on the bracelet, then kissed her gently, sweetly. "This isn't goodbye, Kerry. I'll call you."

After he left, while she stood in the security line, she wondered if he would.

"SIT STILL," Sharon ordered.

Kerry frowned in the mirror at her sister, who was being damn bossy while she put color highlights from a kit into Kerry's hair.

"This is going to look so good," Sharon assured her. "You looked wonderful when you came home from New Orleans. The sun streaks were great with your eyes. Sit still. I'm almost finished."

Kerry sighed and kept her opinion to herself. Her birthday wasn't until Wednesday, which was Valentine's Day, but her parents were holding a birthday dinner for her tonight, Saturday.

For some reason, Sharon had gotten the idea to play fairy godmother and try to turn Kerry into a princess for the event. She yawned as she waited for her sister to finish.

Outside the windows of her cottage, the light glinted off a new snowfall, nearly blinding in its intensity. The sky was a brilliant blue.

Like eyes she'd once gazed into while making love.

She halted the thought as her heart speeded up to a painful pace. True to his word, Matt had called several times since their sojourn in New Orleans. In fact, he'd called nearly every night. If he didn't call, he sent an e-mail.

Except he hadn't done either the last couple of days.

She'd found herself hovering by the phone Thursday and Friday night, then had finally gone to bed, irritated with him for not calling.

However, she had to be practical. As she'd expected, the calls were tapering off. Maybe he would still invite her to New York.

If some of the magic lingered, they might exchange calls again for a while, but eventually they would drift apart. Their communication would come down to postcards from exotic locales where he was researching the new book he'd told her about. Perhaps he would mention someone interesting he'd met.

Ah, well, the life of a celebrity was a lot more glamorous than her life. Not that she wanted to change. She was happy in her job…and in her life… pretty happy…

"Okay, we have to let that stay on for twenty minutes," Sharon said, checking her watch. "Let's pick out something for you to wear. I can't believe you went to New Orleans and didn't buy one single outfit. That just slays me."

"Hey, I bought those clothes you talked me into before I went on the trip."

"Oh, let's look at those. I want you to look really good. You're not getting any younger, you know."

Kerry threw a sofa pillow at her sister. "Thirty-five isn't all that old."

"Speak for yourself. I'm three years younger and I feel ancient."

"Well, that's because you've got kids," Kerry told her with superior logic.

"Isn't that the truth. By the way, they loved the gifts. Ian took the python photo to school for show and tell. The kids declared you and…what was its name?"

"Jolie."

"Yeah, they thought you and Jolie were a great team. They decided *you* were awesome. I quote your nephew."

Laughing, they went into the bedroom. After a thorough search, Sharon selected black slacks, a black fitted camisole with a built-in bra and a black-and-green cardigan to wear over it.

"That looks really good," she said. "Informal but sophisticated. Chic."

"Just the effect I was going for," Kerry murmured facetiously. Right. For dinner with her parents.

Sharon seemed to think this was hilarious.

After a shower to wash the highlighter out of her hair, Kerry dressed and even put on evening pumps when Sharon insisted she needed them for the outfit.

Her sister also helped her with her makeup, adding a golden sheen over dark, smudgy shadows on her upper eyelids and insisted she brush on several layers of mascara.

"Look," Sharon commanded, turning her toward the mirror on the bathroom door.

Kerry blinked at her image. She looked different from her usual self and more as she had on vacation in New Orleans last month—smart and glittery, but mysterious, too, with a smile playing at the corners of her mouth…as if the woman who gazed back at her had a wonderful secret.

THIS IT?" the driver wanted to know.

Matt checked the address again and decided this was definitely the cottage where Kerry lived, just as Sharon had described it to him. The roads had been cleared of snow, and his driver had gotten them from the airport and over the county road without difficulty.

"Sure is," he said, and handed the man a couple of bills. "No change."

The driver nodded in pleasure at the tip.

Matt thought any amount was worth it to get here. The blizzard yesterday had been a worry, but he was here at last.

He was a little surprised to find he was nervous as he walked up to the front door, his luggage in hand.

If Sharon was wrong…if his own instincts were wrong…well, this trip was going to be a disaster.

He rang the doorbell and admired the pinecone-

and-dried-apple wreath on the door. When he heard footsteps inside, his heart went into overdrive.

When Kerry opened the door, all his muscles seized up and his heart skipped several beats.

"Matt!" she cried, her eyes wide and staring and utterly beautiful.

"My God," he said, "you're even lovelier than I remembered. And that's a fact, not a cliché."

"Matt," she said again, blinking rapidly.

"Yeah," he said in a very husky voice, "it's me."

"What are you doing here?"

He gestured toward his suitcase. "You said it was okay to visit any time I wanted. May I come in?"

She was charmingly flustered. "Yes. Of course. I'm so glad to see you…I don't understand…uh, do you want to stay here? I have a guest room."

A blush bloomed like a rose all over her face.

"But you probably have other arrangements," she ended, giving him an anxious stare.

"No. I'd hoped you would invite me to stay."

She stepped back so he could enter and closed the door behind him. He breathed deeply and caught the scent of cinnamon in the air and the familiar drift of rose blossoms from her favorite cologne.

He dropped the bag and gathered her close. "I knew I'd missed you, but I hadn't realized how much until this moment."

Unable to resist, he kissed her, and it was like every

dream he'd had for the past five weeks—no, better, because this was real.

Kerry was sure this wasn't real, but Matt was here. In the flesh. He was kissing her as if he'd really missed her. And she was kissing him back.

"Matt," she said at one point a long time later. "Matt." That's all she could get out, she was that thunderstruck by his presence.

When he lifted her into his arms, she held on tightly, then settled happily in his lap on the sofa.

"This is like a dream. Oh!" she said in alarm.

"What?" he asked, nuzzling along her neck and collarbone.

"Tonight. There's a birthday dinner. At my parents'."

She realized she didn't want to leave home or see anyone else or have to make small talk.

"I know. I'm invited."

He lifted his head and gazed into her eyes, which made her mind go hazy, like she was soaring into an endless blue sky. "You are?"

"Yeah. Is that okay with you?"

To her surprise, a sort of anxious look came into his heavenly eyes. She squeezed him as tightly as she could.

"Of course. I'm delighted, just surprised, that's all— well, actually, flabbergasted," she babbled, suffused with happiness she couldn't suppress. "Oh, Matt, this is the best birthday present ever," she assured him.

His laughter worked its usual magic on her. She glanced at the clock. They should be at her parents in forty minutes. With a fifteen-minute drive, would there be enough time to…?

She realized there wouldn't.

"Uh, we need to leave in a few minutes. I'll show you to your room." She groaned. "I sound like the staff at the Hotel Marchand," she said when he cast her a questioning glance.

Laughing softly, he followed her to the guest room and left his bag there. She pointed out the guest bathroom and invited him to freshen up. Glancing at her reflection in the mirror, she realized her eyes were shining and her cheeks flamed with color.

Happiness, she thought. Having Matt here was the greatest happiness.

But when he leaves? some part of her asked.

She shook her head. She'd think about that when the time came, she decided, and ignored the piercing ache at the thought of another parting. Going into her bedroom, she removed the charm bracelet from her jewelry box and fastened it on her left wrist. There, that felt right.

For an instant she stared at the intricate love knot ring nestled among her small collection of birthstones and costume jewelry. It seemed to glow in the lamplight as if bestowing a birthday blessing on her.

When Matt returned to the living room, she was standing by a side table, waiting. She noticed he'd changed from the casual jeans he'd arrived in to dress slacks and a muted plaid shirt of blue and tan. He carried a tweedy sports jacket of heather blues and browns draped over his shoulder and held by a finger. Oh, but he was the handsomest man she'd ever seen.

"Ready?" she asked.

He nodded. "I'm with you, kid," he said in the tone of a hard-boiled movie detective.

They smiled and simply stood there for an enchanted moment, staring at each other.

He was the first to move. "After you." He held her winter parka while she slipped it on, then opened the door to the frosty winter chill.

To her, the evening air felt as balmy as it had in New Orleans last month. She drove them to her parents' home, still not sure she wasn't imagining all this. Several cars were already in the drive when they arrived.

"Happy birthday," her relatives shouted when she and Matt arrived at the door.

Her grandparents were there, her sister and her family, her aunts and uncles, several cousins and their children.

Kerry glanced at Matt and relaxed. He was perfectly at ease in a mob scene. She grinned and squeezed his arm.

He gave her a wink and calmly shook hands as she introduced him to twenty-three of her closest relatives.

"Let's eat," her nephew suggested after the introductions. "Then we can get to the cake and ice cream."

From that moment, the evening became a blur of laughter, stories—mostly about her and Sharon's exploits—delicious food, and finally the cake and ice cream.

There were presents of jewelry and clothing and handmade knitted scarves, plus a tiny diorama of a nature scene from her nephew and two nieces, composed of a bird's egg in a tiny nest, twigs for trees, dried seeds and pebbles for landscaping, all glued to a round cedar plank.

Matt gave her a sterling silver charm with gold accents. She recognized it as the Hotel Marchand.

"Ohh," she said, then couldn't say another word as he snapped it onto her bracelet. When the evening started to wind down, she found she was ready to go home. She thanked her relatives for a wonderful birthday with hugs and good wishes for them all.

"I'll help with the dishes," she told her mom.

"You'll do no such thing," her mom retorted, shooing her out of the kitchen. "It's your birthday …well, on Wednesday, but we wanted to celebrate when everyone could be here."

"I know." Kerry threw her arms around her mother. "It was a super birthday dinner, Mom."

They held each other for a moment, then her mother said, "Go home with your young man. I think he wants to have you to himself."

Anticipation rose in Kerry. She laughed. "I think I want to have him to myself, too."

Her mother touched her cheek before they rejoined Matt in the living room. "Be happy, darling."

"I will. I am," Kerry assured her.

She and Matt headed home just as a light snow started falling. "Good timing," she told him.

"I agree." He paused. "I liked your family. Your parents made me feel very welcome in their home. And it was nice meeting Sharon face-to-face after talking to her on the phone this week."

"I think I detect some collusion going on between you two," she accused, thinking of her hair and makeup and the outfit that her sister had insisted she wear.

"Uh-huh," he agreed, but wouldn't confess to more.

At her house, she saw it wasn't quite eleven by the wall clock. That seemed a little early for bed on a Saturday night. She turned on the gas logs in the fireplace.

"Would you like some hot cider?" she asked.

Matt shook his head. "Come sit by me."

Feeling a bit startled, she went to the sofa and sat down, careful not to crowd him. When he kicked off his shoes, she did, too.

"This is cozy," he murmured.

"Yes." She could barely get the word out. Nervous, she tucked her feet under her and leaned into the corner of the sofa, farther from him than she liked, but safer. She didn't want to seem pushy in case this visit was more casual than she hoped. She sensed currents flowing between them and wanted him to lift her into his lap as he'd usually done in New Orleans when they were alone.

"I have another present for you," he said after a long moment.

"Really? I can't imagine what else you could get that would please me more than this," she said, fingering the hotel charm on her bracelet. "Plus the other charms you've already given me."

"Can't you, Kerry?" He gazed into her eyes for an eternity, then lifted his hand and opened his palm. "Can't you imagine this?"

She stared at the ring—a diamond mounted in an intricate gold setting. "Matt, is that…"

"An engagement ring? Yes. I hope you'll accept it. Will you?"

To her amazement, he dropped to one knee in front of her.

"Will you marry me and make me the happiest man on earth?" he asked.

Tears filled her eyes. When she lifted her left hand, he had no difficulty slipping the ring on. Once it was in place, he kissed her finger as if making a pledge to all the ring stood for.

"I can't believe this," she said, throwing her arms around his neck. "I didn't dare think that more would come from our time together than friendship and fond memories of our stay in New Orleans."

He got up, then settled on the sofa, lifting Kerry onto his lap, exactly where she longed to be. She nuzzled her face into his neck and sprinkled a thousand kisses everywhere she could reach.

"It was a wrench when you left," he told her. "I wasn't ready to give you up. I don't think I'll ever be ready for that. I love you. You know that, don't you?"

Cupping his beloved face in her hands, she stared into his eyes and saw only truth and sincerity. She nodded solemnly. "I love you, too, but I was afraid to admit it. It would hurt too much if you didn't love me back."

"I do, so that's settled," he said in great satisfaction.

The wall clock chimed midnight. "The witching hour," she murmured. "Matt?"

"Yes, darling?"

"If we marry, where shall we live?"

"*When* we marry," he corrected firmly, "I thought we could spend most of the year here. I'll keep my condo and we can go to New York for the fall. We'll have a wonderful time. We'll catch the new plays, then drive up to New England for the autumn color. In the spring, we'll go to Washington for the cherry blossoms. There's a whole world for us to explore."

"What about your writing?"

"I've finished the latest article and have started my new book. I'll work on it most of this year. When you can take off, we'll go to France and visit some of my favorite wineries there. Otherwise, I'll only need to travel briefly for research. I'll be home so much, you'll be glad to get me out of the house once in a while."

She sat up and gave him an indignant glare. "I'll never grow tired of having you with me."

"I hope not. I plan to be around for a long time. Like seventy years or so."

That made her laugh. "When did you realize, that is…when did…"

"I know that I was madly in love with you?" he finished for her.

"Yes."

"Honey, you had me from the moment you came to my door to help me out."

In the flickering light from the fireplace, she noticed, just before they kissed, the sparkle from her new ring and the warmth that encircled her wrist as the charm bracelet absorbed the glow of the flames. Magic whirled through the room, around them and dipped right down into her heart.

"Patti told me to follow the shining path that would lead from Twelfth Night to the summer solstice," she murmured to Matt. "Part of me wants to be married as soon as possible, but another part wants to wait until June and the beginning of summer."

"We can wait," he said, love and understanding in his eyes.

"Oh, Matt," she whispered and hugged him as tightly as she could.

Much later, from her bedroom window, they looked

out at the shimmering silver path of moonlight on fresh snow that led toward the horizon and beyond, to forever. Kerry's heart filled to overflowing.

Thank you, Patti, Queen Patrice, my-friend-for-a-day, for showing us the way.

HOTEL MARCHAND
Four sisters.
A family legacy.
And someone is out to destroy it.

A new Harlequin continuity series
continues in September 2006 with
DAMAGE CONTROL
by Kristi Gold

Of all the hotels in New Orleans,
he had to choose hers

When Hollywood director Peter Traynor
walked out on the movie Renee Marchand
was producing, his departure ended up
costing her the job she loved.
Now he's checked into her family's
New Orleans hotel and Renee is finding
it hard to maintain her cool.

Here's a preview!

EVEN NOW, Renee was tuned in to everything about Pete.

By the time the doors opened, Renee was balanced on a jagged edge, knowing that in a matter of seconds, they would be alone in her apartment while she tried to maintain a tenuous hold on her control. If he even made one move toward her, she might forget they had enough garbage between them to populate a landfill.

If Pete had noticed her nervousness, he didn't let on when she opened the door and they entered the foyer. He moved beside her and stated, "Very nice," in the calm, collected tone that she'd seen him utilize before, even during the toughest situations.

"The first time I saw it, I knew I had to have it."

"I know what you mean."

Renee glanced at Pete to find him staring at her. Determined to ignore his assessment, she dropped her keys on the chrome-and-granite table set against the wall to her right and opted not to remove her all-weather coat. Getting too comfortable might give Pete the wrong idea, namely that she expected him to stay more than a few minutes.

Leaving him behind, she strode into the living room and pointed to her left. "Guest bedroom and bath down the hall." She gestured to her right. "Kitchen and dining room over there. The doors open onto a veranda."

"Where's your bedroom?" came from behind her.

Not at all an unexpected question, but one Renee intended to gloss over. She turned and faced him, her arms wrapped tightly around her middle as if that could actually provide some charm armor. "Beyond the kitchen, away from the main living areas."

He strolled around the area, his hands in his jacket pockets. "It's a lot bigger than I expected."

Not quite big enough for the both of them, as far as Renee was concerned.

While she kept her back to Pete, a weighty silence ensued as if what needed to be said hung over them like a stifling blanket. Although she'd originally wanted to avoid digging up the dirt, Renee had the prime opportunity to question him in detail about his departure. But to what end? Nothing had changed, and that was the worst part. *He* hadn't changed.

"Just do it, Renee."

She sent him a fleeting look over one shoulder before turning her attention back to the panorama she'd seen at least a hundred times. "Do what?"

"Yell at me. Curse me. Hell, you can even throw something if it makes you feel better."

She faced him again, slowly. "Are you looking for absolution, Pete? If so, I forgive you."

"But you won't forget it, will you?"

She released a mirthless laugh. "Do you mean forget that you were instrumental in my losing respect and in turn, losing my job?"

"I don't understand that. You made your movie and it was a critical success."

He made it sound so simple, when it had been anything but. "Critical success, yes, but not a commercial success. When Garnett-Mason took over, they only cared about the bottom line. And the bottom line was my inability to keep you on the project."

"My leaving had nothing to do with you."

"Really? I don't remember the exact wording of the clause that released you from the contract, but I do remember it had something to do with finding it intolerable to work with me."

"The attorneys chose to handle it in that matter in order to avoid an exorbitant settlement."

"I see. This had to do with money." She fisted her hands at her sides. "The cost for me was incredibly high. But then, I should have known that was a possibility when you ended up in my bed."

His anger showed in the steel set of his jaw. "Do you think that's what this was about, Renee? Our sleeping together?"

"Isn't it?"

"Hell, no. If I could have stayed on the direct, we

would have handled that aspect. The reasons I left were personal and valid. And because of the possible litigation, I couldn't tell you about it back then."

"Then tell me now."

HOTEL MARCHAND

Four sisters. A family legacy.
And someone is out to destroy it.

Of all the hotels in New Orleans,
he had to choose hers.

DAMAGE CONTROL

by
Kristi Gold

Hollywood director Pete Traynor had loved
Renee Marchand and left her, costing her the job
she loved. Now he's checked in to her family's
New Orleans hotel, triggering a lot of memories—
and just as many questions. Why did he disappear?
And why can't Renee forget him?

Available September 2006

www.eHarlequin.com

HM4

SAVE UP TO $30! SIGN UP TODAY!

INSIDE Romance

The complete guide to your favorite
Harlequin®, Silhouette® and Love Inspired® books.

✓ Newsletter ABSOLUTELY FREE! No purchase necessary.

✓ Valuable coupons for future purchases of Harlequin,
Silhouette and Love Inspired books in every issue!

✓ Special excerpts & previews in each issue. Learn about all
the hottest titles before they arrive in stores.

✓ No hassle—mailed directly to your door!

✓ Comes complete with a handy shopping checklist
so you won't miss out on any titles.

- -

SIGN ME UP TO RECEIVE INSIDE ROMANCE
ABSOLUTELY FREE
(Please print clearly)

_____
Name

_____
Address

_____
City/Town   State/Province   Zip/Postal Code

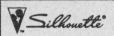

ANGELS OF THE BIG SKY
by *Roz Denny Fox*

(#1368)

Widow Marlee Stein returns to Montana with her
young daughter, ready to help out with Cloud Chasers,
the flying service owned by her brother. When Marlee
takes over piloting duties, she finds herself in conflict
with a client, ranger Wylie Ames. Too bad Marlee's
attracted to a man she doesn't even want to like!

On sale September 2006!

THE CLOUD CHASERS—
Life is looking up.

Watch for the second story in Roz Denny Fox's two-
book series THE CLOUD CHASERS, available in
December 2006.

*Available wherever books are sold, including most
bookstores, supermarkets, discount stores and drugstores.*

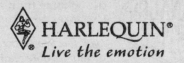

HARLEQUIN®
Live the emotion

Silhouette® Desire

**Introducing an exciting appearance
by legendary
New York Times bestselling author**

DIANA PALMER
HEARTBREAKER

He's the ultimate bachelor...
but he may have just met
the one woman to change his ways!

Join the drama in the story of a confirmed
bachelor, an amnesiac beauty and their
unexpected passionate romance.

**"Diana Palmer is a mesmerizing storyteller
who captures the essence of what
a romance should be."**—*Affaire de Coeur*

Heartbreaker *is available from Silhouette Desire
in September 2006.*